THE HONORIUS HIGH MONSTER BALL

...HAD GROWN TO A monster-sized mash of frightening proportions over the years. No one quite remembered the tradition's origins, but, much like a graveyard, it just seemed to keep getting larger and more inhabited. The Monster Ball Committee went out of their way to make each "Halloween II" an even bigger Halloween celebration than All Hallows' Eve Itself. Black and orange banners lit with thousands of orange Christmas-style lights hung over and around every window and door; most of the halls had the usual fluorescent lighting replaced with ultraviolet, to illuminate the Halloween II Art Committee's eerie paintings and decorations.

Images, sculptures, statues, and carvings of imps and demons, goblins and ghouls, werewolves and vampires and mummies lurked, prowled, skulked, and lay in wait throughout Honorius High. As the first waves of costumed teenagers began flooding in, Mrs. Blair Trundle of the Music Department ensured that the speaker system piped nothing but spooky sounds of creaking doors, yowling cats, howling wolves, and various screams and shrieks.

It was a true temple of the *qliphoth*, the vestiges of forgotten potencies, repressed and relabeled demonic. It was a dark, haunted, hellmouth made flagrant and unapologetic. It was the Enemy Incarnate, flocking with emissaries of evil.

It was high school.

And now, on Walpurgisnacht, as a vast Egg Moon rose in the east, as The Borgo Pass tuned their guitars and tightened their drumheads backstage, it yawned in welcome to Golem Creek's sinister brood...

Also by
DAMIAN STEPHENS

☽ ★ ☾

Letters to an Editor

&

THE MEANS OF ESCAPE TRILOGY

A GOOD YEAR FOR

MONSTERS

THE MEANS OF ESCAPE
BOOK TWO

DAMIAN STEPHENS

FOURTH MANSIONS PRESS
CHARLOTTESVILLE, VIRGINIA

A GOOD YEAR FOR MONSTERS
The Means of Escape
Book Two

FOURTH MANSIONS PRESS, LLC
Charlottesville, Virginia

fourthmansions.com

ISBN: 978-0-578-66015-8

Cover art © 2020 Bryan Baugh
cryptlogic.net

Cover design & text © 2020 by Fourth Mansions Press, LLC
Interior layout & design by Fourth Mansions Press, LLC
Hieroglyphics from JSesh. Used with permission.

Public Domain Materials
Page 56: Yassiz quotes Sir Gerald F. Kelly in an epigraph of Aleister Crowley's
Tannhäuser (*Collected Works*, Vol. I, S.P.R.T., 1905).
Page 185: The title of the epilogue is from Ernest Dowson's poem
"Non sum qualis eram bonæ sub regno Cynaræ" (1889).
Page 189: Also in the epilogue, "Damian Stephens" quotes a few words from
Crowley's *Liber XXX Ærum vel Sæculi Sub Figurâ CCCCXVIII*,
"The Cry of the 4th Æthyr" (1911).
Additional quotations are all from ancient/medieval/Renaissance sources, newly
translated by the author where necessary, and referenced in the text.

For my friends:

Charles Steuart Estes
(1977-2018)

and

Scarlett DeStefano
(2000-2018)

...there is that which remains...

K
V
T
H

PERHAPS IT IS NOT TOO LATE

IX

CONTENTS

☽ ★ ☾

PROLOGUE

☽ ★ ☾

THE
BUSINESS
OF
MAGIC

ANY GIVEN UNIVERSE, IT *turns out, can be a tough nut to crack.*

Things within *it, you see, tend to be forgetful—one reason why the previous book in this series began with the word "REMEMBER" positioned prominently on its first page.*

And speaking of "remembering," I forgot to remind you who I am: Roland, from the Place of Solace—the so-called "Dreamkeeper's Emporium" (a name derived from the combination of Steve, Julie, and Charley's thoughts when they encountered it—I would've chosen something vastly different). If you're reading this, it's because you've been "tagged" by one of the operatives in your world whose job it is to direct paranormal traffic, as it were. And if you didn't read Charley's "confession," that's fine for the moment. Just work with me here, and try to follow along.

You're dreaming this. *Don't worry about it; everyone around you and everything you see—including, paradoxically enough, this very book you're holding,* and even the notion itself—*is part of the dream. Our job is to remind you of this, now and throughout the remainder of the book. You will be reminded of it in many ways, not necessarily direct. By the time it's over, you ought to be well on your way to waking up, possibly for the first time in your life—all the memories of which, of course, are simply dream memories, typically "validated and verified" as "real" by the dream characters in your environment.*

You're *the one we're looking for. The rest of them? They're all aspects of you, anyway, so once we're done, you won't have to worry about them anymore (even if you decide you want to, which is, of course, totally up to you).*

Like I said: the universe can be a tough nut to crack. Everything you believe to be "true" holds only for the moment you're thinking it. This

3

includes by default all the stuff you think is "false" (just another way of believing). So we'll work on cracking this nut together—but I'll warn you right off the bat that what's inside is extremely delicate and occasionally unpleasant to taste.

None of this would be necessary if Charley hadn't set down that confession and started this whole world-crossing affair. I wasn't about to stop him, even if I could; Laban installed me with one of those damned fail-safe mechanisms he and the rest of those practitioners of Old System Magic were so in love with. Besides, I'm kind of interested in seeing someone else's dreaming for a change, if that turns out to be possible.

Let's start with checking in on what's happening right now in Golem Creek:

FRAZZLED, GAUNT TOM FALLOW headed north on Main Street well before dawn. Cloudy as it was, he hoped it would remain dark longer than usual. He could barely see the long bulk of Chicken Hill off in the distance, the orange lights of downtown Golem Creek illuminating nothing more than a shroud of fog.

This suited him well. His usual shift at Morrigan Mfg., the plant halfway between here and Rookville, had suffered the annual hours cut. He worked nights, almost exclusively— eleven to four in the morning. Then he'd drive home to downtown Golem Creek and, before heading back into the hovel he rented for $350-plus-bills a month (at Willow Grove—you've seen it even if you didn't know the name), he'd take a walk over to Main and give himself a chance to absorb his favorite kind of world: one without *people* in it.

That morning, though, on his way past Frick's Rx (where he usually picked up *Tales from the Crypt* or *Fangoria* once a month), right where (usually) there was a brick-walled alleyway that cut straight through to Third Street (convenient for a quick getaway if, for example, you didn't have exactly the right amount of money for the latest *Tales from the Crypt* or *Fangoria*), before the sign that read HARDWARE in big block letters (the one which had never been taken down, even after Elmer Bagsley sold it to his ex-wife so she could start a wig store), he stopped dead in his tracks.

HARVEY'S, the sign above him read, illuminated by hidden track lighting. And beneath that: "*Spells, Spell Books, Paraphernalia, Etc.*"

APPROACHING THE SHOP'S ENTRANCE did little to aid Tom in recovery from his initial shock.

A large display window stood to the right of the door, advertising heaps of extraordinary merchandise. There were magician's cabinets, wands, capes, and top hats, of course, but there any resemblance to your usual illusionist's supply store ended. Elaborate tarot cards fanned out on velvet altar cloths upon which lay basketball-sized quartz crystal spheres on intricately carven wood stands. Talismanic periapts like eldritch images out of a horror movie hung from strips of rough leather and shimmered mysteriously, rendered as they were in bas-relief on shiny, unidentifiable iridescent metals.

Painted in old-fashioned lettering on the window glass and door were advertisements: *Check out our Extensive Selection of Alchemical Remedies! Fortunes Told: Inquire Within (the usual sacrifice fee applies). Ghost & Demon Cages Available! Need a HAND? Hands of Glory (with certificate of authenticity)...*

Tom reeled back, stepping inadvertently off the curb and into the soundless street.

"*What?*" he breathed out, clutching his chest. Something about this had him panicking. An intrusion into his little, boring world...*had he fallen asleep at the plant...?*

He turned around, trying to calm himself, his back to the store. "Okay," he said aloud. "Okay. If this is a dream, then that store won't still be there when I turn around."

He frowned at himself, staring at the little hill of lawn in front of him across the street, at the stone steps of the quaint and quiet Billingsworth Manor Inn, at its darkened room windows. A single cricket chirped somewhere impatiently. *Why would he want it to go away?*

He hesitated to turn around. If "Harvey's Spell Shop" *wasn't* still there, he'd be kicking himself for the rest of his life, having squandered the ultimate solution: *real magic* to deal with all the fakery, all the boredom...

Strange thoughts marched unbidden through his mind. *If there's no explanation for it, then it doesn't have to be...then again, it could be, for the very same lack of reason. Right?*

He breathed out, deeply. It had to be. It *had* to be!

Slowly, he turned around. And, indeed, something had changed.

There was a sign in the window, still swinging gently from side to side.

OPEN, it read.

A CHILL WIND HAD picked up. He stepped through the portal, noticing that the door itself was framed in a pointed archway beset with a fanlight, the numbers *1132* painstakingly inscribed on its marbled glass.

As bells over the door chimed, announcing his entrance, and an indescribably comforting scent of old books and imminent rain enfolded him, he saw, sprawled out in rows and columns and stacks and heaps, a treasure trove of *magic*.

To his left, upon entering, stood the checkout counter, large glass cabinets sporting voodoo dolls and miniature black pyramids and little scrolls tied with fine, hairlike threads. An old-fashioned cash register, the kind with circular keys sticking way up on metal stalks, sat magnificently to one side, right next to a rack of business cards advertising—

"Lycanthropy, Unlimited," he read aloud from one of the cards, this one thick and still smelling of fresh-pressed ink. *Bodies Piling Up? We Can Help! Call Jack — Thurstone 2294.*

He set the card back down in its slot, right between *Familiar Spirits: If You're Not Haunted, We're Not Doing Our Job!* and a mysterious, pitch-black card that seemed, inexplicably, to *grin* back at him when he glanced at it.

He turned to face the shop's colossal magnificence. Thunder clapped outside, a bolt of lightning briefly illuminated the shop window, and the unmistakable sound of showering rain sealed him in.

"I died," he said aloud, his voice consumed by the walls of thick tomes surrounding him. "I have died and gone straight to the starry heavens."

"Almost," said a chipper voice returning from somewhere deep within the stacks.

He jumped. "Hello?" he called hesitantly.

"Hello!" the voice echoed. "One moment. Be right with you."

He stood stock-still, frightened but irremediably curious. There followed a murmuring from the area where the voice had emanated, a low, growling exchange which did little to dispel Tom's lingering anxiety.

He surveyed the scene before him, trying to discern movement from the stacks' deep darkness. Books by the thousands stood, sat, slouched, lay, and curled up on sagging shelves beset with curious symbols, labels, and suspended ornaments. A fantastically intricate spider's web stretched between two stacks of incunabula above him, the characters "$exp\{10^{68}\}$" inexplicably burned into a plank of gnarled wood at its side. Tom took one step back and nearly bumped into an abstract golden effigy bearing the words "MONAS HIEROGLYPHICA" scrawled cryptically on a little price tag hanging from one of its upper horns. To the left of this, an elaborate plaque reading "PICATRIX" sporting images of planets and stars; beneath the word, an arrow labeled "FÆRY COSMOS/IAK SAKKAK" pointed at a long row of what appeared to be candles.

"Færy tapers," a voice behind him said. He jumped again, and out of an obscuration formed from an overhanging, over-sized batwing stepped what Tom presumed to be the shop's proprietor. "Admittedly peculiar method of transmitting knowledge, but of all people, who am I to judge? Speaking of which."

The elfin old man extended a long-nailed claw in his direction. "Harvey Lamb," he said simply, sounding more like a twenty-year-old carnival huckster than could be guessed from his wizened appearance. "And I advise you, Tom Fallow, not to do it."

Tom stared at him, forgetting utterly the outstretched hand of welcome, mesmerized by the shimmering spectacles perched on his hawk-like nose.

"Um," Tom said simply, feeling the weight of the silence upon him. "Excuse me?"

Harvey Lamb shrugged, grinning, and proceeded to extract a pipe from one pocket of his tweed waistcoat. "You've probably noticed our somewhat exclusive catalog," he proceeded, tamping some mossy, dark tobacco into the pipe's bowl with the end of a thin metal lighter. He raised the pipe to his lips, still grinning, and spoke with the end clenched in his teeth. "And it's here, of course. Whatever it is you're looking for."

He sparked the lighter and took several puffs. An unearthly scent of heavy, rain-soaked woods assailed Tom's nostrils. Lightning flickered from windows somewhere farther back within the store.

"Were you just talking to—" Tom started.

He nodded. "Business at odd hours, that's for sure!" he remarked, turning and gesturing for Tom to follow. Harvey Lamb was nearly lost to the flickering, gaslit depths of the stacks before Tom pursued.

"We're looking for...aha! Right," he said, and started left, toward a rickety spiral staircase. Even here, books, weird images, and trinkets overflowed ancient wooden shelves that wound around the walls, following the staircase. "This way."

The sound of pounding rain outside diminished even as the confines of Harvey Lamb's Spell Shop seemed to expand. Tom felt as if he were heading, somehow, *deeper*, with every creaking step of the staircase winding up.

They finally reached a nearly empty landing, having passed several more densely packed floors sporting impossible quantities of merchandise.

"Tom Fallow," Harvey Lamb announced once in the octagonal room above. The visitor's name hung in the air for a moment as he approached one of the windows looking out of each wall. It was—

"Golem Creek," Tom said, astonished. "It's *amazing*. You can see the whole city from up here!"

Harvey chuckled, puffing on his pipe and continuing to grin delightedly as he watched Tom flit from one window to the next. Although the rain and lightning obscured some of it, Tom knew the town well enough to identify its primary landmarks. There sat the neighborhood off by Ballard Park; the foggy precipice of Chicken Hill, home of the Murk, the Wishing Well that he and so many others had frequented during high school, hoping, *praying* that whatever-it-was granting wishes there would deign to grant his; and on the other side of town, the proud and Gothic and wildly inappropriate Honorius High itself. He could even see Laban Black's old manor on Brake Street from here, and at least determine the general area of his own apartment complex amidst the sheets of rain.

"But how—?" Tom asked, breathless. "I mean, I've never seen this place before."

"Tom Fallow," Harvey said again. Tom turned to see him standing before a small, black box, like a miniature treasure chest, resting on a waist-high wooden table overhung with the stained-glass shade of an electric lamp. "You have a choice. You may choose to leave now. You may choose to forget the unseen world you've now seen something of."

"*What?*" Tom exclaimed. "Who could forget any of *this?*"

Harvey's grin faltered. "Some of them wish that they had, later," he said.

Tom snorted. "Like *who?*"

"Tom Fallow," Harvey repeated a third time. "They would like you to help them return."

"What? Who?"

Slowly, carefully, Harvey rolled back the lid of the chest. Tom stepped close enough to see a handful of shimmering mauve crystals resting on folds of black cloth within.

"What is that?" he asked.

Harvey removed his pipe and set it on the table beside the box. He passed an aged hand over the contents. "This is the *ajña* of Yassiz, the Old One," he said, his eyes fixed on the radiant crystals. "The Laughing God. The Incomplete. The Unconcluded."

Tom shook his head in confusion. "What does that mean?" he asked.

Harvey pulled his gaze away from the crystals with

palpable effort, and closed the box's lid. "Would you like a job, Mr. Fallow?" he responded, grinning once again.

Tom looked from Harvey Lamb to the box, then shifted his gaze back to the extraordinary thunderstorm pummeling Golem Creek. It spoke to him—in hammering rain, in reverberant thunder, in flickering lightning. Darkly, it conveyed something to him, sibylline and mysterious and somehow *perfect.*

A means of escape...

From the drudgery of that place—from the *wrongness* of that "real" world...

There was something he could do to fix it.

"Well?" Harvey said. "I'll need an answer now, unfortunately. My employers have insisted that no one leave this place with any knowledge of its existence should the offer be declined—"

"I'll take it," Tom said reflexively. "I'll take it. Now. I'll start now."

Tom found himself breathing a sigh of relief.

Harvey chuckled again, his eyes brightening. "Very good, young man!" He lifted the box from the table and headed back to the staircase. "If you'll follow me?"

Tom followed, realizing suddenly that he didn't know what the job *was.* "Do I need to, um, put in my two weeks at the factory, or something?" he asked.

Harvey's chuckle became a laugh. "You're on the winning team now, Tom Fallow!" he responded. "Besides, all that nonsense about your life before this time has just been, let's say, 'taken care of'!"

PART ONE

☽ ★ ☾

NIGHT
OF THE
DEMONS

CHAPTER ONE

HOT FOR CREATURE

BATSHIT CRAZY, THE SLAVERING beast raised massive fists like knots of gnarled and twisted oak.

Its voice came like grinding stones. *"Where is Damian Stephens?"*

Charley cowered in the corner of the bathroom, feeling the twin pulsations of his heartbeat and the drums from the rave down the hall.

"I don't know who you're talking about!" Was that true, though? Did the demonic metalhead know something he didn't?

The thing—but let's call him by his assumed name, "Edward van Halen"—let out a shriek sounding like thousands of groupies flung at once from a tenth-story hotel window.

Where the battle axe came from Charley had no idea—

JESUS! YOU'D THINK I'D be able to at least hang on to the edge of the plot!

Sorry about that. Backing up...hitting rewind... Wait for it...

All right! Let's put some pensiveness back in the suspense! (That was terrible—I'm going to try it again.) Let's make this "wait" a little more "heavy"...? (Better? Nah...)

JIM THE JANITOR PERKED up when Janice the Secretary strode past his little custodial office on the lower level of Honorius High School, her scent of vanilla and fresh-brewed coffee an invigorating combination of wakefulness and sleep. Jim was hung over again—but no matter. He was at work. And

13

Janice, in a moment of atypical malignity, swish-swished in her polyester bell-bottoms back to his office door.

"Jim? Are you on the clock?"

Jim lifted his hand in a shaky, B-vitamin-deficient salute. "Twenty-four/seven, as they say, ma'am." He wondered at the statement he'd made.

Janice smiled. "Could you head over to the back corner of the playground, maybe, before school starts? Looks like a wild animal killed something back there."

Jim smiled broadly. His mouth once more uttered speech before thought intervened. "Stock in trade, ma'am!"

Janice whisked away, her "thank you" Doppler-shifted in Jim's immaculately polished marble halls. He found himself alone again, standing stupidly in his janitorial coveralls, haunted by the ignoble ghost of Crown Royal.

Wild animal. Huh.

WALTER J. PATTERSON, AUGUST Chief & Principal of Honorius High School, had to call the police a little later.

"Yes! *Body parts*... Well, I *don't know*! Could be... What? Yes. I think so... It was Jim Buskey. The janitor... No! Jim just—what? Fine."

He hung up the phone.

"*Janice!*"

Janice came skipping into the office, smiling broadly as she always did once her morning Valium kicked in. How old was she, anyway? Twenty-five, maybe? What the hell was she so anxious about that she took Valium every day? And where the hell could he score some? His usual gin & tonic breakfast/brunch/lunch/afternoon snack had begun to wear on him.

"Yes, Principal Patterson?"

Probably that goddamned doctor at G. C. General. Pritsker? Whiskers? Something like that. Ridiculous name for a ridiculous man. Only got the goddamned job because his goddamned brother owned the goddamned *Gazette*—

"Principal Patterson? Are you *sleeping*?" Janice gazed with concern at her boss's figure, slumped suddenly, its worn, unshorn face leaning at an odd angle against its worn, threadbare office chair.

"Gah!" Principal Patterson snapped awake, gasping for breath. Janice let out a brief scream, no less sincere for its brevity. "I want you to get that lazy-ass janitor in here *right now*, goddamnit! I got Sheriff Pigmeat—"

"Rigley?"

"—Sheriff Rigley *on his way* to take a look at these *body parts* in the *goddamned playground*!"

"Yes, Principal Patterson! Right away, sir!"

Janice skittered out of the room. Walter J. Patterson barely waited for her absence before opening the right-hand filing cabinet of his desk and pulling out its sole occupants: a finger-printed highball tumbler, a half-empty liter of Hendrick's, and a promise that the day would grow easier as his alcoholic haze grew deeper.

"...TENTH VICTIM OF WHAT appears to be a dangerous new trend among Golem Creek teens. The catatonic youth is under observation at Golem Creek General Hospital. Doctors warn that, despite the recoveries so far, long-term damage from the new drug is still a possibility. In other news: a body discovered this morning on the grounds of Honorius High School is suspected to be that of missing high school senior Kelsey Littleton. Police report that the girl appears to have been the victim of a grizzly bear attack, but the Littleton family expresses outrage at what they have dubbed 'shoddy detective work,' citing the fact that there have been exactly zero cases of grizzly bear attacks in Golem Creek in over fifty years—"

"Barkeep! Another of these fine concoctions, if you will!"

Seated on a rickety stool at CJ's, half-attending the barely discernible words of Channel 9 News, the man calling himself Nashe St.-Demp, Esq., grinned and held aloft his fifth—sixth?—empty glass, tapping it and chuckling delightedly. The barkeep nodded. She called herself "Rachel No-last-name" (as far as Nashe could deduce after questioning) and seemed, for the most part, to tolerate Nashe's occasional visits. She was tall, rather beautiful—part Native American, perhaps?

"Did you know," Nashe started, as Rachel refilled his glass with straight bottom-shelf bourbon, "that the term 'coction' means 'to cook'?"

Rachel shook her head. "Nope," she said simply.

Nashe feigned astonishment and sipped his drink. "As *extraordinary* as the last one!" he said, and coughed lightly into his fist. "What do I owe you?"

Rachel thinned her lips (we might call it a "smile," for Nashe's sake) and wiped rings of condensation off the table. "You're money's no good here," she said.

"In*deed*?" Nashe grinned broadly.

"Yep," she said. "I mean, what the fuck is this? Monopoly money? Did you get this at Toys 'R' Us?"

Nashe shook his head sadly. "Indeed *not*, love. I only wish I had. In sooth, the material means you wave disdainfully before mine eyes is, in fact, the product of honest labor, even if..."

Rachel waited a beat. "If what?"

"Even if 'tis pelf exchanged for falsehoods given in good faith," he finished. Grinning again, he took a healthy gulp. "By the *gods*, what *ambrosia* once hid, now revealed!" He smacked his lips egregiously, earning official placement on Rachel's list of people who ought to die in a slow, humiliating fashion.

Nashe gazed deep into the amber liquid and sighed. "Prithee, any word from my dear, wayward Master Fallow on this docile, common night?"

"He was here earlier," Rachel said, lifting up a magnum of wine and marking it with a wax pen. "Over there talking to Andy."

" 'Dandy' Andrew Sanders?" Nashe said, drawing back in shock. "What on earth for?"

Rachel shrugged and made her way to the other end of the bar, to ignore him as thoroughly as "Dandy" Andrew Sanders and the other six or seven patrons scattered about the premises were managing to do. *Another glorious Wednesday night in a Green Country kicker bar...*

A muffled racket of voices erupted outside, followed shortly by an abrupt banging-open of the front door.

The man who strode purposefully in, his hair half as long as he was tall, made a beeline for the bar.

"Five shots. Pronto," he said, slamming a twenty-dollar bill down on the table not three paces from Nashe.

Rachel set five shot glasses on the bar with Euclidean precision. Seconds later, they brimmed neatly with Jack Daniel's. "Evening, Booker," she said.

Booker downed one shot, grinned back at her, and none-too-carefully lifted the remaining four from the table.

"Be right back. Emergency," he said. He spun around and headed for the door. Almost on cue, it was opened for him by a grizzled-looking, bearded fellow wearing glasses.

"At least whacked his head pretty hard," the new guy said as Booker blazed past him into the parking lot. "I don't know if that will help. He seems pretty incoherent—"

The door fell closed. The entire exchange had taken perhaps three minutes, during all of which Nashe seemed content to stare fixedly into his drink.

"Where, oh, where..." Nashe hummed tunelessly, patting the pockets of a stained army jacket and muttering. " Ὑπ' ἔρωτος καὶ λήθης κρατεῖται...* Aha! Salvation. *Se non è vero, è molto ben trovato.†* 'Thou, Yog Sothoth, seest me.' " He extracted a beaten Moleskine pad and an ink pen that shone with red light when clicked. "*Canis ingens, catena vinctus, in pariete erat pictus superque quadrata littera scriptum, 'Canis Cavem.' "‡*

Nashe thought for a moment, took several more contemplative sips of his bourbon, and finally settled pen to paper, chuckling to himself as he scribbled, scratched, and sketched. Rachel chanced a quick look in his direction out of the corner of her eye. Should she bring him another drink, before he asked for it? Should she bother to try getting him to pay real money this time? Last time was so—*embarrassing...*for him.

This was the worst kind of customer: the one you couldn't

---

* "He is ruled by love and sleep." *Corpus Hermeticum* I.15.
† "If it ain't true, it's a helluva story." Giordano Bruno, *De gl' heroici furori*, II.iii. (*Spero che mi perdoni, O Nolano!*)
‡ "A big dog, tied to a chain, was painted on the wall and over the picture was written in square letters, 'Beware the Dog.' " Petronius, *Satyricon*, "Cena Trimalchionis" 29.1. (By the way: don't ask. I don't quite get it either—not yet, anyway.)

get rid of but you couldn't let stay. *And why was it that she couldn't ever get around to* actually *kicking the bastard out...?*

From his perch at the other end of the bar, "Dandy" Andy tipped Rachel both a five-dollar bill and his hat before exiting with a drunken gait. Almost as soon as the door literally hit him in the ass on his way out, a brief commotion sounded from the parking lot. Earl "Slick Rick" Potoma, nine-to-close regular and de facto bouncer at his seat in the booth nearest the entrance, glanced from beneath his ten-gallon hat at the door, then at Rachel. She shrugged in response. Earl nodded and returned to his beer.

AND THAT'S BASICALLY WHY so many people died that night. Sometimes a commotion isn't just a raccoon getting into the garbage.

"Buck fifty," Tom Fallow said to Weston Gray at their rendezvous point out back. He was usually more talkative, not to mention less jumpy. What was it with him tonight? He had a large bruise covering one side of his face.

Weston Gray counted out five twenties and five tens from the roll of cash Yassiz had provided and handed them over. He noticed in the dim light behind The Flying Monkey that Tom's thin, pale hands shook slightly.

Almost simultaneously, Tom handed him a lunch sack which undoubtedly contained the usual: a few ampules of the ungodly paralytic agent and a handful of clean syringes.

Why he always included the sterile hypodermics was beyond Weston's understanding or concern. Professional courtesy? And the inclusion of a small velvet bag of what appeared to be Valentine's Day hearts imprinted with variously endearing and sickeningly sweet clichés...? How to fathom the queer salesmanship of the criminal underworld?

Tom disappeared into the darkness almost before Weston had taken the lunch sack from him. Weston secured the goods in his backpack, stuffing the velvet bag of hearts in one jacket pocket, then scanned the darkness of the woods behind The Flying Monkey. No movement.

He headed toward the front of the bar where his car was

parked.

"There's the little fucker."

Weston heard the voice from somewhere behind him. *How had they snuck up on him?*

"*This* fucking piece of shit?" A figure came striding up to him from around the corner leading to the parking lot out front. The lights of the parking lot were just barely enough to give him a glimpse of his quarry—

Odd word, that. *Quarry.* Why would he think that?

There were four of them. Two behind, two in front, closing in fast.

"It's Weston *Gray*," said one of them. They looked a little like football players: at least a head taller than him, apparently irascible—the bullying type, at minimum.

"Weston-fucking-*Gray*? Gimme a *break*."

Someone pushed him from behind. Weston stumbled forward. He felt a tingling in the palm of his left hand, where Yassiz had placed the Mark.

Another of the jocks caught him from the front and roughly jostled him back to a standing position. "Look at me," he said. Weston drew in a breath as he did so. "Are you afraid, motherfucker?"

Weston's eyes betrayed the truth: he was not afraid. It seemed to bother the jock immensely.

"Ain't you gonna say somethin'?" This was from another of the victims behind him.

Peculiar word to use in this context. Victim.

The jock holding him reared back with one fist and slammed it into Weston's face. He heard a crunch, which may have indicated the snapping of a bone, possibly his nose. The jocks burst out laughing.

"Yo! What's *this*?" A hand had reached into his pocket and extracted the velvet bag.

"Open it," the jock said to his witless colleague, who proceeded to pour a dozen candy Valentine's Day hearts on the ground. A general chortling of villainous implication arose from the group, sounding to Weston like the bleating of sacrificial goats.

"You gonna keep selling that *shit* out here, motherfucker?" the jock asked. Weston tried to breathe through his nose, couldn't, opened his mouth. The tingling in his palm grew stronger. He lifted his head to gaze back into the jock's eyes.

"What's *wrong* with this fuckin' kid?" Another helpless victim, this one to his immediate quarry's right. "Is he high?"

"He's fucking high," someone behind him spoke. "He's probably on that same shit he sold Mindy. And Becca. And *Jimbo*." There were several indications of regret from the group. One nameless body crossed itself. "The same shit he sold *Kelsey*."

A second blow smashed into Weston's face. He felt his head whip back. He slumped forward inadvertently as the group of ill-fated fools chuckled and hollered, possibly the last sounds they would ever make.

"Look at me," his immediate assailant said again. "You're going to tell me, right the fuck now, what happened to Kelsey. Motherfucker."

Weston lifted his head and gazed into the jock's eyes. *Yes. That's Sturges McCall.*

Something impeded Weston's vision—that would be his own blood. As he noticed it, a third blow smacked into his face.

"Say it," Sturges insisted. The cackling of the jocks was reaching a fever pitch. "You sold it to Kelsey, too, didn't you, you little fuck? You sold it to her—*tell me what you did.*"

"I'd fucking talk right now, if I were you," said another of the hapless victims.

Weston attempted to nod, and took in a breath. He felt raw Power surging through the Mark.

He spoke the Word, exactly as Yassiz had taught him.

"*Avavago.*"

The roaring winds that enveloped Weston were of lightning and fire. The searing heat of a thousand suns enshrouded Sturges McCall and his three luckless appendages.

There was no time for them to scream or rage or fight. There was only that moment of violent ecstasy in which Weston held sway, superbly monstrous, then a peaceful, rotating breeze, fluttering the ashes of the four fools to the four winds, then quiet.

EARL POTOMA ULTIMATELY DECIDED to get a breath of fresh air. Shortly after exiting the front door, he returned in a burst of uncharacteristic liveliness, gasping in shock.

"Y'all oughta take a look at this," Earl emitted hoarsely, supporting himself in the door jamb.

Nashe St.-Demp, Esq., was the last of them to rise from his seat. He drained the final few drops of bourbon from his glass and paused briefly to gain his footing, the floor appearing somewhat closer than he had expected when he stepped upon it. He heard various gasps and utterances implying states of shock, amazement, stupefaction, and wonder.

Rachel stood at the traffic jam in the doorway, peering out. "My God," she said. "What the—dear God, *how?*"

Outside, coruscating whirlpools like sorcerous dust devils shimmered in the dim parking lot lights. Despite bursts of radiant lightning sparking and sizzling out of them, it was the surrounding stillness in the night air that most heightened the twisters' peculiarity.

In moments, the spectacle was gone, leaving only bewildered onlookers in its midst.

"*Accessi confinium mortis,*"* spake Nashe St.-Demp. Rachel turned to cast a pleading glance at him—could he either *shut up* or *do something useful*, like call the cops? Or the Ghostbusters, maybe?

But Nashe St.-Demp was gone. *Id est*, Rachel noted with disgust that the door to the bathroom was swinging shut.

She noted further, after taking several steps out into the cool night-laden parking lot, that a more disturbing aspect of the wild, if short-lived, madness outside lay in the sudden commotion surrounding a body that lay, presumably in a pool of its own blood, on the otherwise unassuming gravel.

"Call an ambulance!" someone suggested reasonably. "It's *Andy*! He's still *breathing!*"

---

* "I approached the confines of death." Apuleius, *Asinus Aureus*, 11.23.

Rachel spun around in time to see, out of the corner of her eye, in the darkness of the forest to her left, a shape within the shadows, dark and malignant, that seemed to vanish into thin air.

☽ ★ ☾

HOT FOR CREATURE
BY
NASHE ST.–DEMP, ESQ.*

Let me begin by alerting you to the blood spattered on this page.

There is <u>blood</u> all over this page, and, what's worse, the classroom is empty.

I have started the lecture, and the <u>classroom</u> is <u>empty</u>!

This moonlight shimmering through the open window beside me, and the chill breeze like grinning death wrapping its shroud around me, begs me to give in, to capitulate, to <u>rest</u>...

And I cannot. I <u>will</u> not!

I will proceed as planned. Perhaps the ghosts of my students grace me with their presence; I would be remiss to withhold from them the experience of this, my final lecture...

It was the summer of 1983, on Earth, the Earth <u>you</u> know, the Earth we all left behind. Summer vacation. I was a boy — thirteen years old, awkward as a first kiss. But smart; I can objectively concede that I was very smart.

And I was very much in love.

---

* Sold for $400 to *Isaac Asthma's Nonstandard Science Magazine*, where it appeared (unabridged) in Volume XXXII, Issue 11, pp. 17-39.

Her name — or, rather, the name she gave me — was Lucy. She came to my window on the second floor of my parents' modest home almost every night for the three months of vacation.

I can still see her so clearly: lavender eyes flashing, blood-red lips barely covering those whitely flashing fangs...

Forgive me. My tears still flow freely when I remember her.

Her visits stopped as suddenly as they had begun, and when school started again in the fall, I found myself immediately attracted to precisely the wrong group of people with precisely the right solution to my problem.

"This chick — what was her name again?" Doug Quince asked. We were smoking a poorly rolled joint in the lot outside Post Oak Theatre.

"Lucy."

"Lucy, right. Anyway: this chick tell you where she lives?"

"You mean during the day?"

"I guess."

"No."

"No?" Doug took a few frantic puffs on what was fast becoming a hazardous roach, hot as a live coal.

"Underground, maybe?" I suggested. "In a crypt, I mean. I think."

"What crypt?"

"St. Albertus, maybe."

Doug nodded. "That would make sense." He offered me the last of the roach. I shook my head.

"That would make sense," he repeated.

The next thing I knew, we were on our way to St. Albertus's in Doug's rusted-out Plymouth. We headed down into the cool, somehow breezy crypt.

And Doug was dead before his body hit the floor.

I stood there in shock. Lucy floated gracefully in a flowing black shroud, her lips stained that bril-

liant, unearthly crimson I remembered so well from
our meetings.

"Lucy..." I could barely whisper. I stood there in
shock. She grinned at me, and came closer...

I awoke the next day in my bedroom with comic books
all over me. I heard someone running a vacuum downstairs. I fell half asleep again for a few moments,
and saw her again, Lucy, her shroud as it wrapped
about me, a last glimpse of Doug's prostrate form,
white and cold, but seeming as if it glowed, smiling
in the dim light...

Then it appeared.

I saw it with a clarity typically unbeknownst to me
in my waking state. My Moloch — my devilish machine —
my beloved's wish come true —

"Henry?"

It was my mother's voice, shouting from downstairs.

"Henry! What is this crap all over the rug?"

I sat up, and dimly remembered. Graveyard earth...

"Sorry, mom!" I yelled. "I'm sorry. I'll clean it!"

I heard my mother growl in disgust. "Forget about
it," she said disgustedly.

I needed a place to work, you see. Lucy had indicated
a mausoleum at one end of Foxend Churchyard, the older

of the two cemeteries in Golem Creek. The tomb itself stank of mold and decrepitude; I would have mistaken it for part of the small hill it was built into, had Lucy not directed my attention to it.

It was perfect.

I began to gather my materials. This proved to be easier than expected, once Lucy instructed me in the dissolution of common morality. That which serves a higher purpose cannot allow the basic proprietary rules of the common folk to delimit it. These were invented, after all, merely to keep <u>Homo normalis</u> in line, and at least moderately organized, but mostly to keep them <u>distracted</u>, constantly checking in...

I stole from the high school, for the most part. The chemistry department, the physics department. As my grades were superior, there was exactly zero interference when it came to unsupervised use. Having completed the majority of my coursework, I had been named "student assistant" in the chemistry department, in charge of deploying all the necessary materials for other students to execute labwork.

I did much of the ordering and organizing of the laboratory materials. It proved easy enough to fake a great deal of this, appropriating much of it for myself, constructing my own personal laboratory in the old dungeon beneath the mausoleum piece by piece...

Electricity was something of an issue. Lucy, however, introduced me to several nameless servitors — ghouls, if you will — wandering in their half-life beneath the streets of Golem Creek, seeking constantly the rot and carrion that formed their primary nutrition. These entities aided me in tapping into an electrical grid via the forgotten control station of a buried, dysfunctional subway system.

I admit that I was shocked and peculiarly thrilled when she told me of the latter. The implications were staggering. There had been a city beneath this city... And it was easy enough to presume the culprit of the interment: Laban Black...

☽ ★ ☾

NASHE ST.-DEMP, ESQ., STOPPED typing (before it was finished) and stopped re-reading (after he received his complimentary copy of the publication issue).

Laban Black?

What the hell was he thinking?

And Dr. Asthma never even blinked. He just bought the damned thing and published it, as sent. It didn't seem like the editors had done much except change the original name of the young mad scientist—Henrik Shaxplay, Ph.D.—to "Henry."

And hadn't the vampire-seductress "Lucy" been named something else in the original?

He had even made the cover art: wild, arcing electricity piercing an old well on a spooky hill. Ghostly forms descended the hill to an unassuming town below, where they would enshroud themselves in mortal forms, to take their pleasure among the living...

The Beast itself, the Thing that Dr. Shaxplay brought back from under the earth, remained a terrifying hint, a monstrosity limned in Lovecraftian metaphors.

Nashe had done it on purpose. That was the next piece he was going to write.

Just as soon as he got hold of Tom Fallow again, with his magnificent confection, wherever he was.

...and a young girl awoke from a dream of a world, vast and seemingly void of all inhabitants...she had placed the envelope where she thought it would be found—but in that timeless realm, when *would he find it...?*

CHAPTER TWO

DON'T STAND SO CLOSE
TO MEPHISTOPHELES

I'LL HAVE TO RE-INSERT *myself here. Many apologies, but trying to direct attention in a linear fashion across nonlinear, multidimensional spaces* looks *like this!*

I was just flipping through the third volume *and it occurs to me that there are several characters involved in this story whom you've barely met. Let me see—oh, right. This is important:*

"ENDURANCE," THE DEMON SAID, licking gore from its black talons, "is what separates gods from men."

Weston Gray sat on an upturned milk crate behind Clark Tumbleweed's silent specialty grocery store and lit a Nat Sherman, listening intently. Heavy clouds of smoke billowed from his lips as Yassiz spoke.

The latter's eyes lifted to heavens dark and fat with rain. Yassiz chewed thoughtfully on the pound of flesh provided by its young disciple, then continued.

"The line between our worlds is not irrevocable," it said. "Who draws it? Your species; your rule-makers." Yassiz chuckled, the deep rumble like a padded box filled with heavy coins tumbling down a staircase. "But they make those rules because *we* have settled them on it. *We* maintain the line."

Weston, his face flat and emotionless, took a drag off his cigarette. "But the circles? The words? The sigils—"

Yassiz interrupted him with more heavy laughter, lowering

---

* The Means of Escape, Book Three: *Zod-Manas Zi-Ba, or Morpheus Unbound*, by Damian Stephens.

the young girl's carcass.

"We *agree* to respect those," Yassiz explained. "We hold to our side of the bargain—it maintains the illusion. But don't think for a moment that we couldn't step through those invisible barriers and have you by the throat."

The creature made its face into the semblance of a grin, and popped one of the girl's eyeballs into its mouth. *Something about those eyes...* Weston thought, his own visage calm and composed. The demon's eyes shone with fiery blue, the pupils never exceeding the size of small central dots, somehow betraying the fact that, no matter what Yassiz said or did, it was *imitating* humanness, making whatever it said palatable to Weston's unfortunate aspect as a member of that inferior species.

"It is for *your* sake"—the creature indicated Weston specifically with a nod—"that we agree to certain terms. In the end, like most things, it's just business." It took another mouthful of brain from the fragmented skull, chewed, and swallowed. "Nothing personal," it said.

Weston took a final drag off his cigarette and tossed it on the ground. It fizzled in a small puddle of leftover rain. Thunder rumbled in the distance.

"I should be getting home," Weston said. Yassiz had returned to its snack with aplomb, the lecture clearly over for the night. It nodded without looking at him, and dragged the remainder of the corpse behind a dumpster. "You'll make sure to—"

"Yes, yes, of course," Yassiz growled. "I'll make sure."

Weston turned and headed out of the alleyway. Downtown Golem Creek shimmered with the lights of orange streetlamps, reflecting off shop windows and rain-slick streets. He turned left onto the sidewalk, toward the South Street light where it intersected with Main.

Weston paused briefly. Perry's Deli Meats was on the corner, and across the street Widener's Beer & Wine. Dragon's Den Bookshop haunted the end of Main, still gazing out at the blank spot where they had razed Post Oak Theatre after the big fire that made it cheaper to destroy than rebuild.

He turned on to South Street. It was a long walk back to the neighborhood district. It looked like it was about to rain again.

That was good. That would help wash away some of the blood, if Yassiz didn't manage to get rid of it all before skulking back off to the woods, or wherever it was that demons went when they weren't setting up their twisted plans.

I'M CERTAIN YOU'RE WONDERING *about everybody else by this point. Where's Charley? Steve? Whatever happened to the lovely Julie Evergreen, stranded in Tulsa with a copy of* Fear Club*?*

In enlightening you about our old friends, I am constrained by the limits and expectations of print media. I must attempt to compress four dimensions to less than three; I must implore your patience as I linearize the dynamic and exponentiated. There were several characters in our story that you needed to know about "first." But hang on—for the impatient, I must oblige, if only briefly:

CHARLEY AND STEVE, BACK in the Place of "Solace," were fed up. Sick and tired. Mostly tired. And now, mostly drunk.

They leaned on either side of a large, granite headstone beset with a gigantic and fearsome manticore. In front of them lay the rest of the graveyard, the vast hole they had dug before the tombstone of "Miller H. Life,"* the grasses and stones glinting in the moonlight. A huge iron grate reading "MORS JANUA AMORIS" in nearly incomprehensible scrollwork lay far beyond. Charley contemplated it from his current vantage point:

ᴹᴼᴿˢ ᴶᴬᴺᵁᴬ ᴬᴹᴼᴿᴵˢ

He wondered what it meant.

Steve refused to share the bottle of Johnnie Walker Blue he'd reserved for the occasion of their failure. It was just as well. Charley had decided to drink Captain Morgan's, anyway, so it all ended up working out.

---

* The tombstone read: MILLER H. LIFE: ONE FANCY FRIEND! DRANK HIMSELF DEAD—'CAUSE LIFE'S JUST PRETEND!

Neither of them spoke for a while, gazing exhaustedly at the questionable fruits of their labors.

"So, that pipeline down there," Steve finally said. "What do you think it's for?"

MEANWHILE, JULIE'S BEEN BORED *to tears working in the University of Tulsa's Special Collections department...*

...WHERE THE IMPRACTICAL DIVERSIONS of her boss kept any real work from getting done. She tried—typically with success—to sequester herself in the holdings of McFarlin Tower, ostensibly cataloging skulls, arrowheads, and the occasional baffling and indefinable artifact.

One rainy day, having braved the silent, hungover houses of Fraternity Row on her way from student parking, she noticed against the dark grayness of the sky something flickering in one of the upper windows of the Tower. And her heart skipped a beat—because of that book, because of *Fear Club*, because of all the weirdness that it said happened to *her*, and the wildly impossible things that it said took place *right up there...*

She made her way to the top floor directly, giving her usual excuse to M— C—.* She ought to be alone enough, at least, to smoke a joint next to one of the wall-unit air conditioners, if the flickering light proved uninteresting.

She found nothing, at first. She climbed some of the rickety metal stairs leading to rows of artifacts on the room's upper level. Rain beat heavily on the roof, its echo reverberating against the stone walls. She leaned against one corner and contemplated the joint in her cigarette pack, idly flicking the lid of her grandmother's lucky Fabergé lighter.

She'd read *Fear Club* over Thanksgiving break at her parents' place in Oklahoma City. She read it because Molly had insisted she do so. That strange light in the girl's eyes—that weirdly intoxicating scent, her voice...

Well, she *had* read it—cover to cover, as soon as she'd

---

* An unavoidable alteration to protect the present author. —Ed.

gotten into bed that night. Thinking about it afterward, she lay there in a daze, the sun rising over a world now deeper and more extraordinary than it was the day before. A story written by a guy she'd never heard of talking about a girl with *her exact name*, not to mention many of her same characteristics. And the weirdness of it—she practically *remembered* Steve Chernowski, and could almost *feel* her way around that place, Golem Creek...

And the story had an entire section taking place right here, in McFarlin Tower. It was right over there—she could see the spot, could see in her mind's eye the shimmering portal where Steve and Charley had leapt through into Laban Black's tomb to escape the Silent Goblin Gang...

She had, admittedly, sought out other books by "Charles T. Leland," but to no avail. She had returned to Gardner's Books several times in hope of running into "Molly," or finding another copy of *Fear Club*—and met with nothing.

Using the suitably profound resources of Special Collections, she had determined to her satisfaction that the only "Charles Leland" who had ever written anything at all was certainly *not* the same one who had supposedly penned *Fear Club*...

She was beginning to think she possessed perhaps the *only* copy of the damned book in the *universe*.

There was no sign of chaos here in McFarlin Tower. There was no destruction; no steps leading up to some mystical escape-hatch into another world with another history and another version of *her*...and despite a handful of torn-out pages in the book, she didn't think she'd really missed anything important.

Except maybe *where*, exactly, Charley had gotten that weird-ass magic sandwich sword.

And there had been no answer when she'd called the number "Molly" had given her. Nothing but a brief pause before the musical three-note alert indicating that she had "reached a number that has been disconnected..."

Julie found herself suddenly burdened by an immense sadness.

LAST I CHECKED, THESE guys were dead, but far south of Julie in time and space, Booker, Barton, Fitz, and Staley—the "Silent Goblin Gang"—seek and find the End of the World...again:

THE HEADLIGHTS OF THEIR green Jeep Cherokee (used for undercover work of this nature, as it handled a little better than the Pontiac out in the country) cast meek illumination over the dark asphalt of Sheridan Road approaching 111th Street. Fitz drove, keeping an eye out for the reddish-brown pole and electrical box that marked the entrance to Murdock's Gate.

"As great an idea as this is, we have to consider the resources necessary," Booker said. "I mean, we're talking about potentially ramping up the network considerably."

"There's *money* in it, man," Barton responded, idly racking the slide on his P30. "That religious cult out in Norman? They'd be like flies on this shit! We could fleece the hell out of those guys."

"It's true," Staley said. His penlight played over a torn map of the area. "Fur oughta hold. If we skin 'em quick enough."

"Hm," Booker said. "It'd have to be *real* quick. And we still don't know if it'd change back afterward." He gazed out at the darkness. "Hey, don't miss the turn."

As spooky as the area was, with shadows deepened by overhanging clumps of tree branches, the Goblin Gang— having braved the villainies of Hell Hounds and Bat Creatures, and sought an audience with the Jersey Devil after that fine gentleman relocated to Lawrence, Kansas, for a time, among other adventures—remained unfazed, especially given the presence of a Chuck E. Cheeze not a mile behind them.

Tulsa became infernal fast.

Fitz pulled the jeep off the road and paused on an ancient broken asphalt drive. Booker jumped out of the front seat before the car stopped, chain-cutters in hand. The Goblins watched as Booker jogged up to the asymmetrical panels of chain-link fence strung together with a length of old steel chain, and made short work of it. He waved Fitz forward, bowing like a maître-d' as they passed through, then hopped back into the front seat.

"Let's see what trouble ol' Murdock can cook up for us tonight!" he said, slamming the door. Staley put away the map and switched off the penlight.

"Who the hell keeps fixing that gate lock?" Fitz asked.

No one bothered to answer.

After the gate, their approach to the ruins was asphyxiatingly silent. No wolves baying, no creatures flitting about, no leathery wings flapping above. Nothing but the jeep's engine rumbling and the sound of Staley lighting a cigarette penetrated it.

"What, maybe twenty, twenty-five a pop?" Booker suggested suddenly, continuing to follow dollar signs in his mind. "We could even sell it to—oh! I know! Remember Amazaz, or whatever his name was? The alchemist guy?"

Barton nodded. "Who else would he get it from?"

Booker chuckled and clapped his hands. "Let's do it! Oughta be some action tonight—"

"Kill kit's in the Pontiac," Fitz said.

Booker visibly deflated. "Well, shee-yit." He sighed. "All right. Next time, then."

They reached an impasse soon enough: a felled tree blocking all progress by vehicle.

Fitz turned off the car. Silently, the Goblin Gang checked their gear and exited. Booker made one further comment before leading them into the darkness.

"Remember the rule," he said, giving Fitz a stern look. "If there's more than one, rack 'em *before* we smack 'em."

THERE! I HOPE THAT *satisfies the paranoids for a moment. Perhaps when the movie version comes out, we'll be able to do this with fewer visible seams.*

Meanwhile, nobody paid attention to Nashe St.-Demp's disappearance from the scene of the crime. Yes, the bathroom door had been swinging shut, but nobody actually saw the drunk leave—although, quite frankly, amidst the sirens and useless ambulances and (for some reason) fire truck that showed up to make the massacre official, nobody—least of all Rachel

Ostenbrennen (she did have a last name, after all)—gave a damn about him.

*A shame, given that—as you probably suspected—he had an enormous amount to do with what was unfolding.**

SOME OF THE HUBBUB, at least, made lunch the next day in the Courtyard (where the smokers all huddled between classes at Honorius High, and less a "courtyard" than a set of forgotten steps leading to a drainage basin behind the school) moderately bearable. Certainly, "Dandy" Andy's assault at The Flying Monkey† was interesting, but the Kelsey Littleton Massacre was like a gift from the Nerd Gods, since everyone had some repressed desire to see a "Honorius Untouchable" get insided-out, so to speak.

"Sturges disappeared?" May Plummer remarked between mouthfuls of Fritos.

Frank Plummer—her fraternal twin—laughed out loud a few steps down. "Probably because he's the one who killed her!"

A general consensus erupted from the little group of twelve delinquent apostles. No love was lost for Sturges McCall or his cronies among this group. His absence was a blessing they all feared to see revoked.

Frank took a drag off his Marlboro Light and began nodding his head. The Plummer twins—like most twins—were weird. Frank wore his grayish blond hair long; May wore hers short. They both had the same upper lip that twisted to the right, affixing a permanent sneer to their faces.

Both also had roughly the same night-black sense of humor.

"I heard she was actually in her room when she disappeared," Cory Benning announced. "Her mom went in: 'Hey, Kelsey.' Her mom left. Her dad comes downstairs, says to her mom: 'Did Kelsey go out?' Mom's like: 'Hell, no, Dad!' And

---

* Please note the appearance of one unavoidable inconsistency in the report of his appearance, *supra*. Go ahead. Look for it. We'll wait.
† Or was it CJ's?

they call Sturges, and he's not home, he's at fucking basketball practice—"

"Baseball," someone corrected.

"—baseball practice. Dad drives over to Pridner and Sturges is out there on the field. Hits a home run."

"Bullshit," May Plummer announced, lighting a second cigarette. After this one they'd all have to head back in.

"*Horse*shit!" Cory responded. "He did."

"No, I mean Sturges," May said. "He didn't kill her."

A groan of dismissal arose from the group. Someone tossed an empty Styrofoam cup in May's direction, which the wind caught and sent hopping on invisible waves into the sky, out of sight.

"How do we even know she's dead?" Petzi Perez (they called her "Peez" for short) asked, glancing up from near the bottom of the steps. Her curly black hair was held back from her face with a blood-red barrette in the shape of a skull and crossbones.

Frank laughed. "Because of the bracelet they found! And the blood on the windowsill where Sturges pulled her out—"

"Sturges wasn't anywhere *near* Bank Street, dude," Cory said.

"I heard there wasn't hardly any blood on the windowsill," Priscilla Rains said from ten steps up. She was a strange one. Supposedly, she had tried to drown herself in Susanne Palmer's swimming pool one summer. When none of the party attendees noticed, she started smashing all the windows in the house. They had a restraining order put on her, in addition to burdening her with fourteen months of community service.

Everyone paused to absorb information and smoke. They all felt somewhat perturbed by what May had said.

"How do you know Sturges didn't kill her?" Peez asked.

May smiled, crumpled the Fritos bag, and tossed it down the steps to the drainage ditch. A light breeze picked it up and scuttled it away. "'Cause I saw Weston Gray that night, sitting in his car at the mall," she said simply. "Watching her leave."

Frank laughed again. "That's so stupid," he said.

"What?" May responded defensively. "You've got a better

idea?"

"Fuck yeah, I do," he said. "It was Priscilla!" Frank began cackling madly as the fourth-period bell rang inside.

Priscilla stuck her tongue out at Frank.

"You wish," he said, stubbing out his cigarette. "Anyway," he continued, turning to Peez as the group began grumbling and standing up, "Priscilla's the only one who knows 'how much blood' there was at the scene of the crime. Plus, she's a fucking psycho."

Peez nodded. "Right," she said. *But how did the body get to the school...?* She separated herself from the group after entering Honorius High through the dark maroon doors at the top of the stairs. She headed in the direction of the soda machines, fully intending to be late to algebra. Reaching in her purse for spare change, she encountered the folded twenty-dollar bill she'd stolen from her mom that morning, the one destined for Tom Fallow.

It was at the end of the hall, just past the Coke machine, that she saw Weston Gray, synchronously enough, standing next to his locker and staring at her. One of his eyes was thoroughly blackened. His nose was swollen and bruised.

Poor guy, Peez thought. *Probably those jock assholes, as usual.*

She smiled at him. As far as she was concerned, he was just a quiet weirdo. Out of fashion, for sure, like he was from the fifties—like that guy in *Rebel Without a Cause*, maybe, if he never worked out. Maybe he had a learning disability. Autism, or something. What the fuck did May Plummer know?

He didn't smile back, not at first. It took him a second, and by that time, Peez had already gotten her Coke and headed the other direction, to the math hall.

"THEY'RE KEEPING IT OUT of the news for some reason, but these were clearly related events," Jim the Janitor informed his friend Bax Laird when they had settled in for drinks at his apartment later that night. "They keep saying it's some new gang in town, but there was a symbol linking the bodies."

Jim typically felt his drunkenness in several stages. First, a strange, wild energy arose within him, followed by loquaciousness, and then, finally, a particular stupor in which various extraordinary revelations were identified, having their foundation in mundane events.

He verged, at the moment, on stage two.

Bax poured himself a liberal dose of some kind of grain alcohol, then added a splash of pineapple juice and sat down to engage his old friend's discourse. They had known each other since (dropping out of) Harvard ten years ago, when they had decided to go into business together back home in Golem Creek. Jim's identification of a growing need for instantaneous communication over large distances using simple, handheld devices seemed like just the thing at the time. Neither of them had figured out a way, unfortunately, to build the requisite device, and the idea had been scrapped along with Bax's emergency plan to build and sell television sets that didn't require cathode-ray tubes to operate.

Bax still felt they would somehow show all those Boston bastards a thing or two. His occupation—as night manager of a FazMart down by Foxend—simply demanded it.

Jim held up a spiral notebook. "This," he said. Bax gazed at the image for a moment, then grabbed the notebook and studied it carefully. Jim, grinning, got up to refill his drink.

"This is..." Bax trailed off.

"I know, right?" Jim bounded back to his seat, almost spilling his drink in the process. "Incredible! There it is: *Khephra*, the Beetle—the Midnight Sun."

Bax rotated the image, angled it, held it up to gather more illumination from the fluorescent light emanating from the kitchen. "This is what they found?"

Jim nodded enthusiastically, the glass of cheap vodka at his lips. "Scratched into the victim in the playground! And decorating the bar's front door, etched in blood by some sort of—let me quote from the paper—'claw-like implement'!"

Bax set the notebook down. "Why would it do that?"

"What?"

"Place the symbol like that?"

Jim shrugged. "Who knows? More importantly, who cares?"

"Well, *I* kind of do, especially since——"

"Hey," Jim made a rapid cutting motion with one hand. "I don't want to hear it. *Even exchange*—that's what they said."

"So they know?" Bax asked flatly. "PYGOLIRO?"

Jim shook his head. "Like I said: who cares?"

Bax sipped his drink calmly. "It just seems a little weird," he said anxiously. "We didn't exactly offer them all that much, if you recall——"

"We offered them *everything*!" Jim drained his glass, trying to hide his agitation. "Besides, it's mutually assured destruction. *He* made that very clear!" He pointed to the palm of one hand with his index finger. "Throwing a wrench in our gears only pulls the trigger on the gun pointing at *them*!"

Bax seriously doubted the mixed, drunken metaphor, but he let it slide.

The two men sat silently for a while in their old complicity. Jim privately recalled his last moment of humiliation. The expensive suit he'd rented; the briefcase he'd borrowed; the business plan he'd painstakingly generated (this one involved an insane notion he called Home Everywhere—a miraculous technology for "autolocating electronic maps")...and when, after being literally laughed out of the conference room by men whose lunch buffet cost more than his yearly rent, he'd simply run downstairs, away, down one flight too many, and discovered a door painted with an Egyptian scarab hieroglyph, behind which lay the Secret of Golem Creek...

Bax reached over and flipped on Jim's Zenith television set. "Crazy Haines is on public access tonight," he said. "What about——"

"*...were no witnesses, though more strange graffiti found at the scene have led police to suspect further unfortunate acts of gang violence. Meanwhile, doctors at Golem Creek General Hospital place the possibility of 'Dandy' Andy's recovery at just over fifty percent. In other news, the latest drug craze among Golem Creek teenagers is easy enough for parents to overlook: Valentine's Day candy, anyone? Three more catatonic youths admitted to Golem Creek General...*"

Jim had stopped laughing. Bax turned to him.

"We've got to kill that guy," Jim said.

"Who? 'Dandy' Andy? The *house painting* guy?"

"How in hell did it *miss*?" Jim asked, astonished.

"Woah, wait a second," Bax said. "Miss *who*?"

Jim shook his head. "Doesn't matter," he replied, setting his drink down carefully. "It's got to be done *tonight*," he continued. "Who *knows* what that guy saw? We can't risk it."

Bax groaned, leaned back, and covered his eyes.

"PEOPLE THINK THAT YOU can just shoot someone and walk away," Tom Fallow said drunkenly. "It doesn't work like that."

The bartender—Rachel Something-or-other, he never quite caught her last name—nodded without appreciation. He realized shortly that she wasn't agreeing with him, merely asking silently whether he wanted a refill.

He tapped the dented oak tabletop next to his glass in response.

"Oh, I almost forgot," he said, fumbling in a backpack on the barstool next to him. "How did I manage to get these?"

He produced four shot glasses and set them on the counter.

"Thanks," Rachel said, removing them to a sink behind the bar. "Why didn't they come back?"

"What?" Tom said, confused. "They're right there."

"Never mind," Rachel said. *This guy shouldn't be drinking. That bruise on his face looks pretty nasty.*

"I got myself in a little fix not one year ago today," he continued without skipping a beat. "Right after I started my new job. I could barely see in all the rain. Walking, I mean. I was walking home when these guys came out of nowhere."

Rachel set down a pint of Guinness and busied herself cleaning Scotch tumblers. Tom could never tell if she was actually listening—he guessed it was some kind of bartender etiquette. Whatever it was, she had it mastered.

"Four of them," he said, rotating the pint glass before him. He watched the Guinness harp disappear to the left and reappear on the right. "Four guys. They looked kind of like—I don't know. Homeless people? Is that what you call them these days?"

Rachel shrugged without lifting her eyes from the sink.

"Hobos, I guess. Which could be true, because they seemed like military types. Maybe they'd been drafted? Skipped out, though, and didn't know Vietnam was over? They weren't that old, I guess. Anyway, one of them says to me, he says, 'Gimme your wallet.' And I'm like, 'Fuck you, man. Get your own goddamn wallet.' And another one, he pulls out this gun that looks like Dirty Harry's—I don't really know guns, you know. I've never shot one. Have you?"

Rachel turned off the sink and whipped a towel off her shoulder. She started drying glasses and peering at them against one of the dim lights behind Tom. Someone smacked billiard balls on the pool table and Tom flinched.

"You feelin' okay?" Rachel said, finally looking at him.

Tom nodded. "Sure, sure," he said. "Anyone seen Nashe?"

The low voice of a newscaster on the little television up in the corner became suddenly audible as whatever nameless country tune on the jukebox faded out. "*...despite the discovery of a bracelet near the scene, presumed to have belonged to the victim, the body is yet to be unequivocally identified. Ken and Marcy remain hopeful that their daughter is alive, and have offered a reward for information leading to her safe return. In other news, Honorius High gears up for its second annual fundraising dance. Witches, ghosts, goblins! Get ready for Golem Creek's Halloween Two!*"

"You think it's linked to 'Dandy' Andy?" Tom asked. His eyes had glazed over—were those tears brimming in his drunken gaze? "You know, Kelsey. That Littleton kid?"

Rachel shrugged. "They're saying he'll live," she said.

Tom nodded dramatically and took a deep breath. "Good," he said. "That's good. I'd hate for anyone to get hurt unnecessarily." He shook his head briefly. "Anyway, where was I? Oh, yeah. Guy pulls out a Dirty Harry gun and points it at me, and one of his friends, this other homeless guy—I could tell because they were all wearing old army jackets and fingerless gloves and shit. Why is that? Did Chuck Dickens start that, you know, in *Oliver Twist?*"

Willie Nelson began crooning from the jukebox, softly. Tom's mind suddenly raced. *Did they know about Harvey's?*

"He grabs my wallet. The guy behind me. Then he pushes

me forward and I slipped and fell."

"Where was this, again?" Rachel asked.

"By Elder, you know? Block past—oh, I forget. East end of town? By Widener's."

"Widener's?" Rachel paused. She had been jotting something down on a beaten-up little plastic clipboard. From Tom's vantage point, it looked like hash-marks, like she was counting something.

"The beer place," Tom said. Rachel frowned. "Anyway, I fell into a puddle and someone—I mean, seriously? Come on! Someone kicked me! Bastard kicks me. I grabbed his leg."

Tom, having almost forgotten his Guinness, reminded himself with several long gulps.

"Pulled him to the ground with me. I'm cursing and shit, trying to crawl up to him and knock his lights out. And then there's a gunshot."

Rachel looked up from the clipboard. "No shit?"

"No shit!"

"Who got shot?"

"Me, of course! That's the whole point of the story! Guy shoots me. But it probably wasn't the guy with the Dirty Harry gun—or, that's what they said at the hospital later. They said it was a little bullet—something like... What is that? A twenty-two, is that right? Guy said—surgeon said that if it had been a forty-four—that's the Dirty Harry gun, you know—if it had been a forty-four, then I'd've been toast. Bled out on the street. Or probably died on impact. Or whatever. Weirdest thing is, they left me my wallet. Didn't even take any moolah—er, Monday—er—"

Rachel burst out laughing.

"What?" Tom was genuinely perplexed. "What's so funny about that?" He took another drink and realized that the glass was empty.

"I'm cuttin' you off, kid," Rachel said, still chuckling.

"Hell, no! I ain't done yet!" Tom stood up and almost immediately collapsed, saving himself from total embarrassment by a clever (if drunken and stupid-looking) pirouette around the barstool. "I mean, I'd like another. Please."

"Tell you what," Rachel answered. "Hand over two twenty-dollar bills from that wallet you didn't lose and I'll think about it."

Tom smiled, extracted his wallet, frowned briefly as he counted its contents, and handed her a fifty.

"Keep the change," he said.

"Earl!"

Tom looked suddenly astounded. "What?"

The bouncer had Tom outside the bar in less than a minute.

"You can't kick out your patrons! Not without a warrant!"

Earl looked down at Tom staring back at him from his vantage point on the gravel parking lot. "Have a good night, son," he said, and went back into the bar.

TOM QUICKLY FORGOT HOW he'd gotten from the parking lot to the street, down the center of which he now stumbled, remembering... *Wasn't this the spot? Wait! Wrong time—wrong place! Goddamned dreaming's all goddamned fucking fucked again—nonono—*

"HEY, DON'T GET DISTRACTED," Booker said, wiping blood off an oversized combat knife onto the creature's Hawaiian T-shirt. "I still want pancakes later."

There had been six of them—all with similar styles, this time. Their leader had been the fastest. He rode a sort of banana/trickboard hybrid. He had a pack of Camel Lights in the front pocket of his tropical-themed overshirt, a faded 1983 *Show No Mercy* concert T-shirt under that, jams with some sort of convolvulus design printed on them, and the expected pair of Converse All-Stars.

Oh, and his hair was perfect. Between and around the pointy wolf-ears, and to either side of the massive, murderous jaws, that is.

Fitz and Staley tossed the final body—which typically took some time to revert to human form after death—on a makeshift pyre they'd built about thirty yards away from the ruins of Murdock's Mansion. Barton doused the conglomeration in gasoline and Booker proposed a toast—some complicated pun on being dodgy and bewhiskered, hardly anyone was paying attention by that point—before igniting it with the proverbial lucifer, post cigarette-lighting.

"They're barely getting into town now," Barton said as the four of them trudged back to the jeep. "Why do they keep coming around here?"

"Let's just be thankful they do," Booker said. "I mean, that's almost seventy-five grand we're throwing in a fire."

Fitz started laughing as he sparked the engine. The bonfire probably wouldn't attract much attention; it rarely did. Most people just assumed it was the usual Worst Possible Thing, i.e., Idle Youth—and most people out here knew that ignoring certain things usually kept you safer than the cops would. Besides, they had figured out how to contain it. From a distance, it looked a little like a campfire. The smoke rose through tree branches and dispersed quickly in the night sky.

They'd stop at CJ's, of course, before heading to IHOP for breakfast. CJ's had been their post-hunt tradition since the night of the Hell Hounds—although, that night, they'd had to use the secret knock and some extra cash to get in.

None of them expected the nutcase wandering in the middle of the road a mere thirty feet from the CJ's parking lot. So we ought to give Fitz a little leeway when he slammed on the brakes late, and happened to tap—*tap*!—the poor bastard, who went reeling off into a drainage ditch.

"Oh, give me a fucking break!" Booker yelled.

"What was that?" Staley exclaimed. "Was that a—"

Barton instinctively drew his nine millimeter and was half out the door before the others saw what he was doing.

Booker followed quickly. "Don't shoot him yet, dude!" he yelled. "Let's at least make sure it's not Fanboy. Can't shoot Fanboy yet!"

Fanboy was Booker's nickname for the "poor kid"[*] who wanted to join the Goblin Gang. Fanboy[†] often demonstrated

---

[*] Actually a thirty-two-year-old millionaire game designer spending most of his days sleeping off hangovers in his unassuming Jenks mansion and most of his nights bar-hopping.

[†] One Karl Gordon Blackburn IV, according to his social security card—

his affection for the rakish hoodlums* by paying their tab at the end of the night.

The Goblin Gang loved Fanboy, but were sure to insist that he wasn't quite "monster hunter material" yet. What they meant by "yet" was "ever"—but what a mean thing to say to the poor kid, especially at the end of the night?

"It's not Karl," Booker said. "It's—"

"Is that Fallow?" Barton asked. He leaned toward the prostrate form. "Yo! Tommy-boy! You all right?"

Fitz started laughing. "Dude! Somebody take his wallet again—"

"That was an innocent mistake," Booker said. "How the hell was I supposed to know he wasn't Stek?"

"It's true," Staley added. "That fucker's almost never where he's supposed to be."

Tom groaned as Booker gingerly rolled him onto his side.

"Sorry about that, dude," he said. "Are you all right? Can you talk?"

"Is he conscious?" Barton asked.

"Barely," Booker said. "I think I should run inside and grab a few shots."

"Is that the best idea—" Barton started.

Booker patted Tom's pockets, lifted his wallet, and extracted a twenty.

"Drinks *should* be on Tom tonight," he said, springing up and racing across the street to CJ's.

Tom, dimly aware of the activity occurring around him, had already begun to forget how he'd gotten there, or why he needed Nashe's help as much as Nashe needed his. Instead, anxious thoughts of magical camouflage pecked at the forefront of his mind, along with an urgent reminder of his upcoming appointment behind The Flying Monkey with Weston Gray, one he *wouldn't* miss...

---

and I can tell you only that the name was, indeed, a fake.
* An epithet for any group of characters who push the plot along. Q.v., "ragtag bunch of misfits."

CHAPTER THREE

RUNNIN' WITH THE DEVIL

"THEY ARE A NECESSARY consequence of life, consciousness, and intelligence—which is, of course, in all cases artificial."

Wise Nerds, Ph.D., rested in his "secret" office—the one he'd cleverly built and concealed within the walls of a row of shops along Main Street in Golem Creek. It had taken a substantial amount of haggling with the entities that "owned" the spacetime configuration thereof, and an unintended (but nonetheless gratifying) empirical validation of his most staggering theoretical discoveries—not to mention almost six hundred million dollars of his inheritance (a pittance, in the long run, but still)—to accomplish. But he had done it. From the look of it, no one would consider it a wonder of the world, nor (as it most certainly is) a wonder of the multiverse: wood-paneled walls, one bare table with two chairs set beneath a window (utterly invisible from the outside) displaying a view over Main Street, several racks of bookshelves bearing priceless first editions of Wise's beloved science-fiction paperbacks, a refrigerator, a microwave, a coffee maker, some cabinets and shelves bearing various foodstuffs, plates and cups, a row of Christmas lights on the far wall, a couch that could be folded out into a bed, a modest-sized flat-panel television set of his own design facing the couch.

Basically it was a research scientist's bachelor pad, and it was a replica (for the most part) of the room he'd lived in for a time during his stay in Prague, where he'd first met the man whose lecture he presently recalled.

47

That was, of course, many years ago, back when Wise had the look of a youthful Richard Feynman about him. Of late, Dr. Nerds might have been mistaken for Emmett Lathrop Brown, and would indeed have been flattered at the comparison. And now, waiting for a sandwich delivery from Fred's—an *au jus* roast beef and mayonnaise served on a palatial estate of the most deliciously greasy fries you'd ever encounter—Dr. Nerds lay stretched out on the sofa and faded in and out of the throes of memory.

"Their positions tend to be semi-random," the lecture continued in his head, cerebro-photographically recorded during the acquisition of his second doctorate (this one in mathematical physics). Henrik Shaxplay's voice rang out crisp and clear, the trace of German ancestry still accessible in its slight modifications of double-u's and v's, the play of light and shadow still as exact and nuanced as the day of its "first" occurrence. "We have, however, in our modest science, determined methods of tracing vibrational overlays."

Dr. Shaxplay cleared his throat and traced several quick sketches on the board in yellow, red, and blue chalk. "The classical methods still retain a degree of usefulness. We would proceed by analysis of radiographic data, in general. Oscillatory configurations can be multiply rendered as a simple orchestration of various wave types." He made another few sketches. Wise grinned unconsciously as his old mentor inscribed an epsilon that he would, in a moment, scratch out and replace with a gamma. "Fourier analysis provides a key to the first phase—"

Several beeps sounded, along with a flashing red light above the door. Wise waved his hand at the door and the flashing stopped. A panel in the center of the door slid open. On a tray in the midst of it sat his dinner. The room was instantly filled with savory and delicious scents. He opened his eyes and sat up.

Moments later, an old episode of *The Outer Limits* playing low on TV, his gaze directed out the window to rain clouds gathering above Golem Creek, he found himself immersed in the consumption of a true sacrament, a real credit to this incredible city. No matter that it all existed as a confluence of probability waves functioning as "real" matter and energy; no matter that it was all held up, so to speak, by its own boot-straps—an interior geometry whose landscape provided its own answers, its own rationale for "being."

The whole realm of so-called "solid-state" physics could, after all, be dramatically mapped mythopoetically. Demons and various creatures of mickle might but narrow purview were simply materials and media, mathematically constrained to do the bidding of the sorcerer by way of circuitry, a conflu-ence of transistors, resistors, diodes, capacitors...

The sandwich, the fries, the whole drama of life as it unfolded beyond this room, as Wise Nerds apprehended it, was good...or at least very interesting.

Such a shame that portions of it would have to be deleted in short order.

He cracked open a can of ice-cold Vanilla Coke from the refrigerator. Its taste, combined with the first few drops of rain falling outside, decided him. Perhaps there was a way to undo the world-crossing that compromised Shaxplay's legacy without utterly destroying its perpetrators? What skill and artistry would be demonstrated by methods of brute force? Avoiding the latter was, after all, one of the primary motiva-tions for his coming here, for setting up shop in one of Shax-play's "little" unintended experimental consequences.

He took a gulp of Coke and leaned back in his chair. Rain began falling more heavily. The traffic scuttling along Main seemed to speed up a bit, harried by the weather and growing lateness of the hour. He ran a long-fingered hand through silvering hair, which had only recently begun to thin.

So Laban wants to wake up...and Curwen wants to keep meddling...

But what about those kids out there? Charles Leland had almost figured it all out! Would it really be the worst thing if they—

Even thinking it bothered the ghost of Henrik Shaxplay, who turned sharply to gaze at Wise in his mind, paused in time, yet no less admonishing. *You don't know the whole playing field...* Wise heard the words mentally once again. *Because if you did, you'd go mad. The door of death is hallowed to those who possess the Key...*

And Nashe? Are you there? Because, really—"Wise Nerds"? That's just *unfair!*

UH—LET'S GET BACK TO *the excitement! Poor old Wise is clearly letting the stress of an I.Q. twice the size of a Utah wives' club get to him. What's next? Ah, yes!*

DUST SIFTING DOWN LIKE snowfall from the ceiling.

Julie sneezed briefly, then laughed. She had taken something—what it was, she could barely remember. Aspirin? Cough syrup?

Oh. She was pretty high—it had been something else, a small piece of paper. Colorful. And this joint was really strong, too.

The dust sifting down from the ceiling was accompanied, at intervals, by a soft, almost comforting thudding noise. She was, after all, in her apartment—right? People walked around sometimes, upstairs...

But there wasn't an upstairs, was there? This was—this was a garage apartment. She was somewhere in...Maple Ridge? Wasn't that an elementary school? Her neighborhood?

She giggled again. The thudding. The dust.

Might as well be back in kindergarten. That was amazing. Hadn't she met Steve then? But that was when he went by a different name. He was so cool. He could fall down on purpose and get sent to the nurse's office. He'd wink at her on his way out of the room. She always laughed along with everyone else.

And that one Halloween, the one with the big rainstorm, after school. Steve had given her his umbrella when he saw her waiting outside for her mom, who was late. Suddenly, this shadow was over her, and the rain was a sound instead of a stinging coldness.

He leapt away and slipped in the floodwaters off the curb, laughing.

The shimmering in the Tower.

Julie started, having crept into a waking dream. *That shimmering. Had* she seen it?

What had she just been remembering? Somebody named—
Oh. That was from Fear Club. *My God, why in the world—*
And what the fuck *is that* goddamned *banging noise?*

Not the dull thumping from above, but the sudden, insistent banging from below, caused her to cry out in shock.

THE FACT THAT MOST so-called "secret societies" are both useless and uninteresting when offered up in context with the rest of the world never seems to put a damper on their awesome, delusional powers of sheer self-interest. This is doubly true when such a society actually holds the key to vast magical powers, commanding mighty forces—those who, with a mere hand-wave, can reduce whole cities to rubble.

Such a group of ne'er-do-wells was known to several popular conspiracy theorists—Golem Creek's own "Crazy" Jack Haines among them—as "Pym's Golden Lightning Rods" (or PyGoLiRo for short). No one seemed to have any clue who originated the name. Their designated emblem was supposedly this:

 $\mu o \varrho \varphi.$ $^{\exp\{10^{68}\}}$ $\sigma \tau o \iota \chi.$
$\boldsymbol{7}$ AL. $\boldsymbol{1}$ So. $\boldsymbol{8}$
KV πR^2 TH

According to sources like Jack Haines, those who saw it, embossed on heavy card stock and posted in strategic locations around, e.g., the University of Tulsa and Golem Creek, typically thought it was a notice for a chemistry club. They ignored the encrypted devices appearing below, advertising specific times and places of meetings.

The alleged announcements physically disintegrated shortly after said meetings began. This miraculous event also went unnoticed by most.

The President of "Pym's Golden Lightning Rods" rested by the fire in his usual plush leather seat at the White Lion, an authentic British pub with a steep entrance fee. It stood in a partially remodeled Victorian mansion on a hill halfway (in a sense) between Tulsa and Golem Creek.

The Treasurer, Prince Harold,* stood and, trembling with rage, spoke first. "I move that Molly Furnival be impelled to make amends for damages done!" He gazed furiously at the fifteen unperturbed men seated around him, their ten-thousand-dollar suits looking even more expensive in the dim light.

"She has broken a sacred trust!" he continued. "Fouled an attempt at Aligning the Spheres! Given a gibbering Nothing in exchange for Something!" (Here he implied what the rest of us would refer to as the playing of a practical joke, of which he himself proved to be the proverbial butt.)

Several murmurs followed this exhortation. Prince Harold retrieved a cigar from an ivory box on a shelf behind him and trimmed the end.

"And your prescribed course of action?" Baron Holger asked innocently, despite the wink he gave Sir Reginald, which latter stifled a laugh.

"There are other Queens of Færy," Prince Harold said simply, grinning and lighting his cigar. "Ones with, perhaps, less...willfulness about them."

The President spoke then. Something about his voice always startled them, as if they never expected to hear such a thing from such a creature—altogether too soft and soothing to pass through that fangéd maw. An occasional brightening of his glowing red eyes was typically enough to shadow forth his intentions.

"What of her motivations?" he asked. "With all we have given her, to act in such a manner—do you not think it peculiar that she find reason to sully the rewards of our agreement?" He paused briefly to regard the barely discernible nods of acknowledgment around the room. "Gentlemen, I bid you consider her motivations."

The nods and glances at one another became murmurs of acquiescence.

---

* All names of PyGoLiRo members are approximate.

Prince Harold's sharp, reptilian features stiffened. "Then how precisely do you suggest we proceed?"

The President signaled to one shadowy servant standing at the ready beside him. The latter proffered a glass of crystal filled halfway with a thick, ruby liquid, which the President received and sipped elegantly.

"Perhaps," he said slowly, swirling the liquid in his glass, which glinted in the firelight, "perhaps there is a Jester we might suitably employ in the proverbial manner." He grinned, sending chills through his ancient cohort. "After all," he added, sipping silently once more, "it seems to be a good year for monsters."

MEANWHILE, CHARLEY'S HEAD HURT. It was a sign, he was sure of it—a sign that he had had *way* too much to drink.

They had left their work—"strategic" digging, suggested by Steve's analysis of the lay of the land from a literal pipe dream (it had been pretty good hash, Charley had to admit)— and decided to crash at a motel two blocks from the cemetery. The place looked like an abandoned relic from the 1950s, and, indeed, the television sets played nothing but black-and-white reruns of old sitcoms.

He took a shower. He tried the vibrating bed, which seemed merely to spread the pain of his aching back so that the rest of his body could share in it. Finally, he took out the little green bottle Roland had given him. It was labeled "MIRACLE ELIXIR!" He drank it.

Then he woke up, headache gone, pain gone, feeling magnificent.

Another "day" had passed. Steve was probably still asleep in Room 1, up near the check-in area.

Charley spread the curtains and looked out at the parking lot, the line of trees at its edge, the wooden fence behind which rose handfuls of cookie-cutter houses straight out of some suburban film set. The strange, fitful sun lighting the Place of Solace cast its final mauve rays over the vast emptiness.

He turned back to the television set he'd left on overnight.

The Munsters played out its opening sequence softly, casting a grayish glow over the floor and against the foot of the door, where a small, unassuming envelope lay.

"What the...?" Charley said aloud. He picked up the envelope and turned it over in his hands. It had his name on the front of it, looking vaguely sinister in light of its context.

He tore it open.

Inside was a single sheet of paper bearing a hand-drawn map of what he deduced to be Golem Creek. There was Honorius High; there was Chicken Hill; there was his house—Julie's, Steve's.

And there was the Brake Street house, as unassuming and quiet as the rest, save for one small feature. An arrow pointed to it, coupled with a single word.

PORTAL.

Wets seb cuah?!?

WESTON EYED THE SMALL group from the back edge of the parking lot. *Another girl.* Yassiz had been quite specific. *Bring me another girl. Something chaste.*

There were four in the group. One was Brandy Vale.

That was the one. Weston had overheard her boyfriend complaining earlier in the week. *She just keeps leading me on and on, dudes! I mean,* seriously!

He had watched them meet up here several times before, Brandy Vale and her boyfriend, the gawky and insistent Larry Garfield, accompanied at the Golem Creek Mall Food Court by Larry's protégé or accomplice, Thad Fulton, and the latter's outlandishly beautiful consort, Stephanie LaPlace.

The trauma poor Stephanie witnessed at her good friend Amanda Whitfield's party last fall had driven her into Thad's long, muscular arms as surely as fire roasts pork.

But Ms. Vale was another matter entirely.

The group began to disperse. First, as always, Thad and Stephanie departed, following whatever erotic meteorology determined the motions of odalisques and bondservants.

Next, it would be a pleasant, entirely innocent stroll along the path through the woods behind Visitors' Field for Brandy

Vale and the entity that accompanied her.

Weston had a strong feeling he would have to do something about that fool in order to deliver the goods to Yassiz tonight.

There—there they walk, arm in arm, headed out the doors at 8:30 PM, same as always...

Relaxed and breathing easily, Weston filled one syringe with an ampule of Tom Fallow's extraordinary paralytic. He became suddenly content with his position as Fate's invisible agent, restfully ensuring the unfathomable purposes of the Laughing God.

He followed them into the woods.

YASSIZ BARELY SPOKE FOR several moments after Weston presented him with Brandy's paralyzed body. Quivering with anticipation, Yassiz sliced here and there, generating a sanguinary flow that only seemed to quicken and deepen some infernal demonic thirst.

Finally, he rent several solid tears in some of her softer flesh, after which the girl's breath came spasmodically, then not at all.

Weston attended to the feast for a few moments, and finally took a seat, shrouded in the shadows of a copse of trees near Visitors' Field.

"Exquisite," Yassiz rumbled. The demon seemed to emanate an ethereal luminescence. He paused momentarily, breathing deeply in the pine-scented night air that had begun to chill with the sun's descent.

"It is good to know that you have made use of the Mark," he said simply. Seated on a felled log with Brandy's eviscerated torso splayed out on his lap like an infernal TV dinner, Yassiz looked almost like something lovable.

Weston took another drag off his Nat Sherman, then gazed down at the palm of his hand. *He* could see it: the sparkling opalescence beneath the skin of his left palm, the elimination sorcery activated by intent. Larry Garfield was nothing more than dust, now. He had fought, somewhat awkwardly, after Weston's abrupt appearance had shattered his hopes for a last kiss from the lovely Brandy Vale.

"Like all the best things, it improves with use," Yassiz continued. He skewered a nameless organ with one claw and lifted it to his mouth. It glistened, dripping blackly in the dim light of a lamp hanging from a telephone pole some yards away amidst the trees. "It seems a short leap to the conclusion from precedent that things being actively regulated must possess some power or potency which threatens an established order."

Yassiz closed his eyes as he savored the viand. He chewed for a moment. "This holds true *even if* that power is imparted to them by way of their prohibition."

Weston gazed impassively at his mentor. What was he getting at?

"At least, that is how the engine runs in *your* world," Yassiz said. He turned back to Brandy's remains and began hunting around amongst her viscera. "In mine, the rules are reversed. Indulgence increases energy. Fire cools and water burns. We make rules so as to shatter them, to discover new, further laws within them, then beat against these new restrictions with every ounce of guile and strength." He slid his talons beneath Brandy's ribcage, staring into Weston's eyes as he spoke, working free the unbeating center of her lifeless rhythm.

A meal, nothing more.

"We live outside the boundaries of unbreakable commandments," Yassiz spoke. Something about the statement resonated within Weston's mind, cracking open some gate within him that entered on old dreams. Yassiz held the dripping muscle in his palm between them. " 'None but the dead can know the worth of love.' "

Weston lit another cigarette as Yassiz grinned, bowed his head briefly in obeisance to Brandy's sacrifice, and indulged himself.

YOU MAY RECALL THE *party in Forty Winks, at Amanda Whitfield's.* It rocked. It rolled. It kicked ass.

It was a killer party. Literally.

---

* The central event way back in Book One. As if you'd forgotten *that*!

But how could Amanda Whitfield's little sister have known what her innocent endeavors wrought? Addie Whitfield had been in the attic with the Ouija board again, trying to ignore the incredible chaos from below, trying to concentrate on the messages while maintaining her trance.*

She sat in the midst of a magic circle, the one outlined in that strange book she'd found the week before. The shapes you must use / In blood drawn / And the abomination of desolation / By great moonlight discover'd...

What did it even mean?

One less night of boredom than otherwise, basically. She certainly felt different, like something converged upon her, now. And the new dreams she'd been having since finding the book—of an incredible, seemingly tenantless place...and leaving clues for some ghost of a person she could only sense, not see...

The Ouija board had led her more in the way of frustration than anything else.

Usually, these things didn't work at all. But she could often get the planchette to slide around on the board for a while, freak herself out, imagine that she really received messages from somewhere Beyond...

She was getting a little tired, though.

Addie stood up in the midst of the circle. The hammering beat of the bass from downstairs reminded her, relentlessly, of where she could not— read: did not want to *—go: see her idiot sister drowning inexistent or self-created sorrows in tequila and rum once again, only to be consoled by her imbecile friends as she wept over a toilet bowl.*

"Bullshit," Addie said. As she attempted to step out of the circle, she froze.

Something had just landed on the roof.

From whatever-it-was there arose such a clatter, Addie found herself perplexed—what was *the matter?*

Simultaneously, downstairs, the indications of general good cheer turned to paroxysms of terror.

"What the fuck is going on?" Addie tried to step out of the circle, and hit a wall. An invisible wall. It glowed briefly, then returned to the void

---

* Her parents had the cutesy notion of naming their daughters similarly: Amanda, the elder sister, and Atalanta, the younger, who bullheadedly insisted on being referred to as "Addie," disparaging her father's nine months of painstaking forename research.

again when she stepped back.

Addie tried fruitlessly once again to cross the boundary, her frustration mounting. The clattering on the roof rose in pitch—it sounded like something was trying to dig through the roof—

There was nothing in the book about literally not being able *to break the circle. She grabbed the dark little octavo volume. Howling erupted from somewhere within the house.*

As much as she welcomed any interruption of the Bee Gees, the disturbance had Addie flipping pages in terror. "There's got to be something here—"

Gunshots rang out below, coupled with the sounds of partygoers fleeing. Addie noticed that the scrabbling at the roof had ceased, and tried stepping out of the circle again.

The invisible wall was gone.

She ran to the dormer window at one end of the attic only to freeze, her eyes wide with wonder and fear. Some thing—*bat-winged and terrible—flopped insanely against the moonlit night sky, away from her house.*

"No fucking way..."

The first thought in her mind after following the demonic interloper's unpracticed flight beyond her line of sight made her laugh aloud.

That was the best thing that's happened to me, ever!

She grinned, lifting the book before her and kissing its warped, cracked, leathery cover. She would be heading back to the house on Brake Street again for sure! If this innocuous-looking treasure had been abandoned there, who knew *what else she might find!*

From the Notebooks of
Michael Flowers

A HEADY MIST COVERED *the road and everything when I arrived.*

I had left the carriage driver about two miles back, in keeping with the Prohibitions and Sacrifices. As I walked, along a path barely more than tadpole-filled puddles at places, the air and the forest seemed to close in around me. The buzzing and chirping of insects began roundly to affect my senses. I felt certain that the various Things of which Curwen had warned stood guard—indeed, that they might reach out to me from just beyond the Veil...yet, instead of dread at the potential and very real violence of their evil touch, I felt as if they goaded me forward, barely holding back a sinister mirth...

The Carter residence announced itself subtly, like a host of wealth at a gathering of parasites. Old, decrepit—there were signs that it had been inhabited recently by vagrants. I approached the tottering structure slowly, basking in another sort of radiance: the presence of the Ancient Ones.

For here I could feel it as at no other place! The far-flung spaces gated by Yog Sothoth seemed to seep through some occult interstice...

...and I followed this peculiar, astral scent to the woods beyond the house, through the ever-darkening, ever-deepening ancestral woods beyond.

To the Den.

By rumor, this Den was the habitation of a great many terrible serpents and other poisonous denizens easily controlled by the devils and demons of forgotten legend. They fed here; they feasted and fornicated and fought here. Here, at the base of a Great Tree that grew down, into the Earth, its infernal leaves and branches nourished by some dark version of our common Sun.

The roots of it were difficult to untangle, and at several points on my way deeper into the cave I found myself, as it were, trapped—often accompanied by the spine-tingling chittering of dozens of unholy vermin, nesting somewhere here, in the dark. At last, I glimpsed it: the pulsing, faint mauve glow of the Sigil, the seal & covenant of my Fathers with the Ones Beyond.

Apprehensive nonetheless, I bided my time, carefully uncovering the dirt-encrusted stélé and marveling at its excellent condition—this, the glorious, exhilarating recrudescence of an Abomination whose time, at last, had come.

I prayed to it in my own way, falling to my knees, overcome with the giddy release of a day's exhaustion and travel—worth every ounce of suffering! The promises had been kept! The Great Secret—the unraveling of the Night of Time!

All of my many concerns fell to dust before that bestial icon. It remained only to complete the sacrifices...to find Her, the One who had eluded me, and eluded me still... I thought I knew where to look.

But I would ask His Dark Blessing first.

PART TWO

☽ ★ ☾

DAY
OF THE
DEAD

$ $ $

THIS SEGMENT OF THE SERPENT

IS PROUDLY BROUGHT TO YOU

BY

MINDWARP ADVANCED™

$ $ $

I DREAM OF JULIE

THE SOUND OF SIRENS, always, in the distance. They huddled in the cold greyness like a flock of pigeons and ached for nothingness. No one disturbed them; no one could, for they had hidden themselves in the midst of the world. For not shunning it, it shunned them; they were entitled only to the barren building, the unwanted earth.

Then the Beast; then the Game. The box from the city that never was.

"He's holding out on us."

Stark claimed to have been in a War. He had scars; he limped. No one doubted it. Besides, he had an army jacket with the name "STARK" stitched over the heart in serious -looking letters.

"Why show up, then?" Marigold asked, her one remaining eye ornamented by a birthmark in the shape of her namesake, her golden locks matted but tame.

Stark smiled. "To own us," he said.

Marigold was silent.

"Look," Stark placed one cold hand on Marigold's thin, tired shoulder. "We find out by following, right? Like always."

Marigold nodded. "Like always."

She shifted to gaze out the screenless, glassless window. Grey sky. Sirens.

AWAKENING TO FLAMES, NO screams heard, no shouting. Stark lay crumpled at the other end of the room.

It was a welcome warmth that night, despite the apocalypse.

Marigold rested for a moment, thoughtful, gazing at Stark, at his body, lifeless from this distance, or from any. Not breathing.

She pushed herself up, sat silently for a moment.

The box.

It lay on its side, several inches from Stark's dirt-encrusted hands. It looked like he was still reaching for it.

Marigold crawled, then stood, a little shaky, not too bad.

The glow from the inferno raged just beyond the room. She could see by its light; she could reach him.

She could lay hold of the box, and did so.

Tears came unbidden to her eyes. She rested one limp hand on his rough, unshorn cheek. He was smiling. She could imagine it.

She stood and stepped, softly, to the window.

It was a long way down. Long enough.

Marigold propped herself on the ledge like a flower, legs swinging, the night air freezing against them.

She tipped forward and saw the world, briefly, like a mirage.

The wind picked up and carried her to safety.

Didn't it?

EYES CLOSED, SHE STILL felt the breeze on her skin.

It was cool, now. Not freezing—just cool.

And someone was patting her face, gently, with small, dry hands.

"Mistress?" the voice was plaintive but pleasant. "Mistress? 'Tis time to awaken thee."

Her eyes fluttered open.

A ceiling, white. A fan pendant, rotating.

A little man, gray-bearded, grinning contentedly, stood beside her on the luxuriously costumed bed.

"Mistress?" he spoke again, his smile faltering slightly.

"Um," she said. She pushed herself up on her elbows.

A room. A girl's room. A *teenage girl's room.*

There—cushioned window-seat, diaphanous veils of frilly white parted before it. There—a Victorian-style desk, painted with a floral motif. There—a vanity, beset with myriad perfumes and beautifying potions.

Though what she saw in the mirror of that vanity from her position on the bed, she noted, pleasantly surprised, did *not* require "beautifying."

It was, quite inexplicably, *her*—but, at the same time, it was not, *could* not be. *Something about the eyes*...yes, that magnificent lavender, still the same strange fiery magic, indelibly *there* no matter what the rest of this palpable illusion insisted.

The little man waited patiently beside her, standing back at attention now that she seemed to have noticed him again. Standing, that is, no more than twelve inches in height— perhaps less, given the sturdy soles of his little buckled boots.

"Victorious Lady!" he announced, bowing low and sweeping his tricorn cap before him majestically. "I am thy humble servant, Farmer McNabb the Elder, of the Gallinaceus Tumulus. I pledge to serve Thee, Glorious One of the Seven Stars, with my life if need be—and most happily, I might add!"

He rose once again, slowly, grinning.

He noticed both her blank stare and his own nervous perspiration, and cleared his throat politely.

"Victorious Lady!" he began again.

"Wait," she said, and pulled herself up to a sitting position. The little man faltered on the shaken mattress, but quickly regained his footing. "What do you mean?"

"M'lady?"

"I'm—" she paused, glancing about the room for something, *anything* with which to orient herself. "Who are—I mean—"

The little man—Farmer McNabb the Elder, presumably, though how she would ever convince herself that this dream was a reality fell now strictly, utterly beyond her—grinned once more.

"Ah, it was to be expected, I suppose," McNabb said. "The spell can be like a weight upon Thee. Forgive me, Your Highness!" He cleared his throat once again and produced a tiny dagger from his coat pocket. "Grand Lady of Færy! Wisest Bride of His Majesty, Our Unnameable Father! If you would allow me?"

He brushed the index finger of her left hand lightly with the dagger. Silently, she lifted it toward him.

"Forgiveness, M'Lady," said McNabb, expertly lancing the tip of her finger with the dagger. She winced. McNabb produced a small handkerchief and absorbed the droplet of blood. He shut his eyes and appeared to be whispering something under his breath, holding the scarlet-stained handkerchief to his lips like a lover.

And Molly Furnival knew herself at that moment, utterly, completely. She, the forgotten queen; she, whose memory of the Good Folk was their very existence; she, a mere girl, a mere goddess.

It was Golem Creek, then. Old haunt.

But there was something new here.

"Oh," she said aloud, and breathed deeply. McNabb's grin returned. He bowed deeply again before her. "Oh! *This* place!"

McNabb began nodding vigorously. "Indeed, Fair Lady! Indeed! We rejoice at your return!"

Molly found herself smiling. She swung her legs over the edge of the bed—briefly, a moment of nauseating fear returned, a memory, of slipping from the ledge of an abandoned building, and—

"Wait," she said, standing up. She noticed for the first time what she wore: a single large nightshirt bearing the faded image of a unicorn rearing its head among the stars—*fitting, that*!

McNabb looked up at her from the bed with concern. "Your Highness?"

Molly gazed at her hands, sensing the warmth of her body, the calm scent of geranium somehow emanating from her flesh. "The box?" she continued. "The box. What—where is it?"

McNabb bowed low once more. "Forgive me, Your Graciousness! I am unaware of this 'box' of which you speak.

Do you wish for me to retrieve it for you?"

Molly frowned. She glanced out the window at the city of Golem Creek, sprawling out before her. *A queen in her castle*—

"Never mind," she said, and strode over to the vanity. "Bring me my maidens. Tell the others to prepare. There will be convocation tonight."

McNabb leapt nimbly from the bed, landing gracefully on the rug. "As you wish, my Queen! It shall be done."

He waited for a moment, hesitantly. "Shall I procure for you anything further, Your Majesty?"

Molly grinned at herself in the mirror. "Something to eat," she said. "Something I like." She waved her hand without giving him another look. "You are dismissed."

The familiar brief scent of burnt marshmallow followed his teleportation from the room.

"So long as I forget nothing," she said to her reflection. *But where is that damned box?*

NASHE ST.-DEMP, ESQ.—WHO HAD realized long ago that simply placing a few letters after one's name conferred deference from audiences who might never otherwise grant you the time of day—sold his first short story, "Parallax," to *Fantastic Fiction* magazine for $350. He was seventeen years old, and it was the largest sum of money he had ever seen at one time.

He spent it all on comic books and cigarettes.

The editor of *Fantastic Fiction* had asked to see more. *Your story*—"Parallax"—*really had us all on the edge of our seats! You've got a real knack for ambience and situational comedy, something we haven't been getting quite enough of in the sci-fi/fantasy genre. We'd love to see more of your work! Please send future submissions direct to...*

Nashe was about to leave for college that summer. In fact, he *did* leave—but while his parents thought he was working hard on a degree in engineering physics, he was actually busy sleeping during the day and writing short stories by night on an old IBM Selectric typewriter. The apartment he lived in—a block away from campus—was very cold and very roach-infested. The superintendent, a Vietnam-war veteran who watched television constantly, repaired nothing.

He hated it there.

Three months later, after submitting seventeen stories to various publications, no less than the incomprehensible Dr. Asthma of *Isaac Asthma's Nonstandard Science Magazine* accepted "Laboratory Cocktail" for publication. Dr. Asthma purchased it for $200 on the condition that he cut a single reference to a maniacal robot. The editor also included a polite request to see more of Nashe's work.

Nashe felt a bit underappreciated by the paycheck. This discouragement was quickly annulled the following day by three further congratulatory letters coupled with three more checks. Over the course of the following two weeks, Nashe received notifications and checks for the remaining thirteen stories he had submitted.

Nashe celebrated with an expensive bottle of red wine and a large pepperoni pizza. Brimming with enthusiasm, he wrote another short story before dawn that day—"A Genius Among the Mole-People"—which he submitted (after sobering up somewhat and fixing the baker's dozen of typographical errors) and sold for a whopping $600.

He became a regular contributor to *Isaac Asthma's Nonstandard Science Magazine.* He also failed his first semester of college, promised to do better during a subsequent probationary period, and succeeded in failing his second semester.

The school pulled his grant money. His parents expressed their frustration and disappointment via answering-machine message and letter.

Nashe St.-Demp moved into a new apartment almost exactly one year after selling his first story. He suddenly found himself with a *savings* account in addition to a checking account. Readers now asked about him specifically, inquiring as to when his next story would be published—or would he perhaps be making any appearances at local comic book shops? Was he working on a novel, by any chance?

And that fall, just before Halloween, Nashe decided to Go Out.

This was a momentous occasion, as Nashe hated Going Out, reserved most of his shopping for the wee hours of the morning to avoid seeing other humans, and had forgotten the names of the few people he'd bothered to speak with in high school and during his first and only week of college. The occasion was sparked, however, by what Nashe considered to be a Good Reason, *viz.*, he had read over his last several stories and noticed something exceedingly peculiar about them: *he didn't remember writing them.*

This mild shock was emphasized by sifting through copies of the many magazines he'd been a contributor to over the last six months. "The Hemlock, Please," for example, had an extended sequence of apparently useless dialogue in which the *Hexerei-Meisterin*, in a moment of atonement, attempts to convince Pushy Simms (the hybrid offspring of the Creature and a high-school girl named Mirabelle) that a mysterious Door exists in the library of Tulsaville College (a contrivance of Nashe's) which could provide a means of escape from his impending slavery to her coven.

"The Ballad of Cannibal Corpse" had some editorial oversights: screen directions, as if someone prepared the story for filming, lodged neatly between other portions of the narrative. But at least those made sense; looking back at "A Good Year for Monsters," he found extensive, inexplicable descriptions of a manor-house in a city utterly devoid of human habitation, leading the reader to a revelatory glimpse of a certain Nameless Book. The mere reading of the text occasions an "opening of the Gate" by which a horde of infernal entities invisibly invades the very world of the reader of the story...

But it was on a sheet still rolled into the Selectric that he found a clew* which he decided, on the basis of the peculiarity and its synchronicity, he ought to follow:

> Jane took a drag off her cigarette and pointed at the shimmering pool of darkness behind the back door of The Flying Monkey.
>
> "You've got to be kidding me!" Chaz yelled, shaking his fists in the air. "It's been here all along?"

---

* *Sic.* This particular orthography blends the concept of a "relevant detail" with that of "a thread to follow."

Jane nodded. "You and Finn have got to get with the program," she said. "If the prison's all in your head, why not just 'pretend' to escape 'for real'?"

She was halfway through before Chaz thought to follow her. "But how do you know where—"

It wasn't finished, yet. But the strangest thing about the scene was that he knew—*knew*—he had not written it.

He did, however, know where to find The Flying Monkey. It was where he'd first run into Tom Fallow, who'd introduced him to what a *real* "gateway drug" was.

Nashe grabbed his latest notebook and put on his jacket. The connection was absurdly obvious. And if Tom wasn't there, he could at least get a few drinks in him and see about finishing "Make Room for IAK SAKKAK." That one was sure to make the cauldron bubble over.

JULIE STOOD AT THE window, gazing out. Rain fell in sheets, blankets, comforters, and, finally, down-stuffed duvets. The stomping on the roof? Presumably a tree branch, weighed down, perhaps detached now. At any rate, it had stopped the moment she heard—

Someone banging at her door?

That was a bit less explicable, given the body laying on the patterned concrete between her apartment and the house it sat behind: the Garrys' place. It was a man, certainly; dark hair, glasses, leather jacket, jeans. Pale—growing paler by the second, given the bloodstain spreading beneath him.

Julie stood and stared. Various presumptions and imaginings kicked and prodded her. *Help the poor bastard, Jules!* something screamed within her. *At least call a damned ambulance!*

But she hesitated. Perhaps she should get a closer look?

She ran down the stairs and peered cautiously out the four-paned window in the front door. There he was—the part she could see of him, anyway. Jeans and combat boots. Unmoving. Unbreathing?

She unlocked the door and, taking a deep breath, pulled it slowly open. A mist of rain wafted in. Lightning paired with an almost immediate peal of thunder burst through the deluge. Julie jumped, anxiously, and finally peered around the edge.

He was staring at her, holding his side, blood seeping out from the wound, washing away toward the muddy flowerbeds on either side of the cellar doors of the Garrys' house.

The man—the young man, as he couldn't have been much more than her age—made an obvious, conscious effort to call out, lifting his head and pointing to her. Julie froze, terrified, rain drenching her to the skin.

He moaned, shut his eyes tightly, and collapsed.

"Well, shit," Julie said. "Shit."

A light went on in the main house. Pete was home. If anyone would know what to do, Julie felt sure, it was Pete Garry. He was as solid as they came.

She crossed quickly over to the back door and knocked.

THEY NEVER FOUND OUT what happened to "Dandy" Andrew Sanders—assistant manager of his father's house painting business (Biff's Paint—a name as interesting as the job), divorced semi-proud father of one and not-at-all-proud father of another one, unwitting visitant of a rogue Chaos Servitor who had clearly (albeit incorrectly) identified his scent as belonging to one "Tom Fallow"—and here's why.

When Jim the Janitor and his colleague Bax Laird sobered up enough to drive on the night they discovered a fault in their stars, Bax thought perhaps they would have to smother the guy, like assassins always did in the movies. Jim, however, set him straight.

"We already have an undetectable means!" Jim reminded him. They were sitting in the Golem Creek General Hospital parking lot, gazing up at the building and wondering how in the hell they would find one comatose man among the hundreds of rooms, especially given that he could awaken and potentially give away the whole game at any moment.

Bax sighed heavily, realizing he was in no way sober, and that his lack of the Mark clearly put him at Jim's dubious "mercy."

Bax noticed Jim's left palm had already started glowing.

"Jim?" Bax said, concern rising in his voice. "Jim! Are you doing it?"

Jim returned his gaze to Bax, whose eyes bugged out in terror. "What the hell?" he asked, then noticed the Mark on his palm brightening. "Oh! Shit. Sorry." He shook his hand out like a lit match. The Mark dimmed.

"That was weird," Jim said.

Bax was breathing heavily. "Does that happen when you've been drinking, or something?"

"Maybe," Jim answered distractedly. He looked back over at the hospital. "I hope I can do this without knowing his exact location. Let me concentrate."

Jim closed his eyes. A moment later, Bax heard the soft susurration of words spoken in the stillness. The mauve glow emanating from Jim's palm returned. Bax sat there, half-drunk and half-paralyzed with terror. From Bax's perspective, the atmosphere seemed to change in some indefinable way. At first, he felt things shift slightly, almost like he was slipping into a pleasant dream; following this was a sensation far less pleasant, a tremendous anxiety, like being chased by some nameless horror in a dark wood...

In Golem Creek General Hospital, "Dandy" Andy dreamed fifty shades of gray. They colored walls of an unfathomably vast chamber surrounding him; he could barely contain his bliss when a crack appeared in their midst, and a rainbow of light flooded through. *Billiard green! Xanthic yellow! Luscious purple, even!*

The extraordinary hues spread out before him, all-consuming...he left only a few wisps of scattered dust and piles of debt for this wretched earth behind.

Jim opened his eyes as the glow in his palm faded.

"It's done," he said, grinning. "Let's go get a burger!"

STEK JARRY'S FINAL THOUGHTS had been these: *Huh. Must've been a portal malfunction, or something. But were those gunshots? Wait a* fucking *second—*

He felt certain, moments later, that he was effectively dead.

Well, this is just burnt bread.

He couldn't move, but after a bit, he realized that it was because he was bound up in some way.

Could he see? He experimented. Too dark to tell. It certainly *felt* like he was opening and closing his eyes...

Bumping around. That's definitely happening.

And a car engine? Slowing down...stopping. *The brakes need some work.*

Doesn't matter, does it? You could be dead, and you're still thinking about whether you'll get to work on time, or whether your killers are going to get a goddamned oil change soon.

He was, it turned out, in the trunk of a station wagon, wrapped in a large plastic sheet. Flashlights held by his captors proved this to be the case, as they lifted him out and began to tie something further to him.

Bungee cords? With weights of some sort?

Aw, fuck.

What struck him most of all was the silence. They didn't speak. Their movements were rehearsed; they knew exactly what to do. *All right, Jocko, on the count of three! One! Two!*

He had imagined the voices, of course. It made the sensation of hitting the water somewhat less terrifying. Perhaps the cartoon versions he imagined would drag him out momentarily, laughing hysterically at his flabbergasted expression. *Gotcha!*

No.

Unfortunately, Stek drowned, cursing the day he had ever trusted those *motherfucking monster hunters...*

"GET HIM WHATEVER HE asks for. He'll be hungry."

It was a voice he recognized. A girl. *Molly's* voice.

Stek opened his eyes.

He lay in the most comfortable bed he'd ever known, wrapped in the softest blankets imaginable.

"Good evening, sir."

A little man beside him spoke. The man, dressed in miniature bib overalls, puffed jovially on a diminutive pipe. His white beard and hair were neatly combed. The rocking chair he sat in creaked softly.

Stek took a moment to appreciate his environment more fully, and sat up on his elbows.

"Where...?"

"M'lady the Queen has instructed me to gather for you what comestibles may satisfy."

"Huh?"

The man coughed politely and hopped off the chair. "Would you like something to eat?"

Stek gazed wide-eyed at the cottage that surrounded him. It looked for all the world like a picture in an old book of fairy tales.

"Um. Sure?"

The little man nodded and scurried off.

It was a one-room affair: kitchen, hearth-stove, small dining table, a few comfortable-looking easy chairs with tables beside them. Some parts of it were absurdly small; others seemed fashioned for the average build of human. Several windows looked out on what appeared to be a spring day, somewhere in a pleasant wilderness.

Stek hadn't noticed where the little man had gone. The room was plainly empty of people except for himself.

Stek sat up and swung his legs over the edge of the bed. He had, apparently, been cleaned and dressed in fresh clothes: jeans, a black T-shirt. He wondered who exactly had done the cleaning—which immediately had him thinking of Molly—

Stek stood up and almost banged his head against a low-hanging portion of the ceiling above.

"Careful, sire!" The little man had re-appeared, bearing an ornate silver tray covered with the "comestibles" he had promised: two double cheeseburgers, an order of large fries, and a twenty-piece box of Chicken McNuggets. "Will this be acceptable?"

Stek barely nodded before diving into the food. He sat on the floor—impeccably clean, it proved—and immersed himself in the gravy of life. Hunger, it seemed, had been more than a moderate neglect since—since—

The little man hefted a Super-Sized Coke onto the tray.

"Where am I?" Stek asked, leaning back against the base of the bed. "Was that Molly Furnival's voice I heard a moment ago? How long have I been here? Who are you?"

The little man sat back in his miniature rocking chair by the bed, produced a match, and re-lit his pipe. He took a few puffs of the fragrant smoke, which shimmered in the air between them. Stek took several deep breaths and closed his eyes. *Damn, the food was good...* He reached for more fries.

"You may call me Dunsany," the little man said at last. "Many questions I know you have. That's good! But fear not. She will return before long." He puffed again on his pipe.

A memory of leaping through the portal in Golem Creek suddenly blazed forth solidly in Stek's mind. "Did they—"

"They did," Dunsany said. "They did. But you need not fear them. You are as safe as can be here."

Stek paused a moment, sipped his Coke. *As safe as can be?* "Am I—"

"No," Dunsany responded before Stek could finish his question. He patted Stek on the knee reassuringly. "Eat. Rest. She will return before long."

The little man got up from his chair and strode confidently to the door of the cottage. Stek noticed that there was a smaller door, identical to the larger one, set into the larger one's base.

"How do I contact you if I need something?" Stek said earnestly before Dunsany reached the door.

Dunsany pointed at a call bell on a credenza by the door. "Ring that," he said, and stepped out. The fragrant breeze of a cool spring day wafted into the room as the door swung shut.

Stek gazed down at the empty box of fries on the tray. "Should've asked for a beer," he said aloud. He stood up again, and noticed an eight-pack of Guinness resting innocently on one of the tables, a full pint glass beside it glimmering in a ring of condensation.

"Not bad," Stek said. He immediately began to think of what else to ask for.

AND STEK AWOKE MUCH later to the fresh-falling rain and a

thunderclap.

A shape, dark, humanoid, its countenance suggestive of trolldom, pounded heavily on a door several paces away.

Wryneck...? The word echoed in his mind inexplicably.

He saw the thing evaporate in a stroke of lightning. The pain in his side returned.

Oh, I get it. That was one of those near-death experiences. Right. Well. Beware little men and their too-good-to-be true promises. Beware Chicken McNuggets in a fairy cottage. Goodbye cruel world, and all that...

A girl's face peeking at him through the rain was the last thing he saw before blackness.

"YOU'LL BE FINE. BUT don't mess with my stuff while I'm gone."

Stek opened his eyes. Again. *I recognize that voice. Is that—*

"Mom and Dad are going to be in Switzerland visiting Uncle Augie. So you'll have the house to yourself."

Stek blinked slowly as the room came into focus. "Pete?" he asked hesitantly.

It was Pete—but not any "Pete Jarry" Stek had ever considered possible before. *This* Pete wore a maroon Polo shirt, khaki slacks, and—dear God—were those some kind of expensive leather *dress shoes*?!?

"Don't interrupt me. Brittany's driving me to the airport. I planned on breaking it off with her last night, but this damned merger provided *yet another* distraction." Pete sighed and slung what appeared to be a violently expensive messenger bag over his shoulder. "Anyway. I'll do it when I get to London."

"Um, *Pete*?" Stek broke in again. He sat up in a bed—*his own* bed, but how he knew that was at present beyond him—and felt a dull ache assert itself where once a bullet had lodged in his left side.

Pete was in the process of exiting Stek's bedroom. He turned around abruptly, the look of annoyance on his face intensified by several rapid glances at a Rolex on his wrist. "*What*, Stek? Do you—oh, of course. The credit card's on

Dad's desk under the blotter. *Please* try to avoid getting shot again. Dr. Nishitani insisted that this was the *last* favor he would do for me. Not to mention that it took another chunk out of your trust fund—"

"No! Not that! I—" Stek suddenly realized that he didn't know what to say, suggest, ask, or utter. He decided on a suitably boring cliché. "Have a—have a nice trip."

Pete was out the door without another word.

"Okay," Stek said aloud. "Okay. All right. This is the second—third?—time you've woken up. All right. This is just another part of the death process. Must be."

Stek got out of bed and stood up. *Death is so much fucking weirder than I ever thought it would be.* He wore a pair of silk boxers and a T-shirt bearing faded lettering: *Never Mind the Bollocks, Here's the Sex Pistols!*

TWENTY MINUTES LATER, HAVING decided to get dressed and creep down several flights of stairs to a posh kitchen on the ground floor, Stek saw the girl from the rainstorm leaving what appeared to be a garage apartment behind the house.

"Well this is unusually consistent," he said aloud as he watched her head to her car, an old Honda Civic, curse briefly as she threw a backpack into it, and then return the way she'd come, having apparently forgotten something.

Maybe I ought to talk to her? Even as he thought it, whispers of recognition began to present themselves in his mind. *She's... she's a college student. Here. Here in...Tulsa? Oh, Jesus, I'm back here in Tulsa, Oklahoma...*

The girl—was it Janie? Julie? Julie!—returned to her car, a cigarette throwing plumes of smoke around her, hopped in, and drove off.

"So...this is the part where I borrow Dad's car and follow her?" Stek suggested to the empty house. The presence of a family photograph of the Garrys' "star boy"—at least in this universe—Peter James "Garry" (according to the embossed calligraphy beneath it) wearing a suit and tie, and bearing the most shit-eating grin Stek had ever seen, made the decision for him.

That and the utter lack of any prominently positioned photographs of Stek himself.

The four-car garage had three cars in it: a slick, black Porsche, a HUM-V, and a nice, economical Toyota Corolla with a few dents and scratches in it.

Stek found exactly one set of keys hanging near the garage door. The fact that the keychain bore an old Star Wars logo was proof enough that he would in no way be driving in style that night.

Figures, goddamnit. Can't even get a break in a parallel universe...

He got behind the wheel of the Toyota and was in pursuit of Julie perhaps five minutes after she'd left, fully intending to return "home," if only to ransack the place. *If I can't find the keys to that fucking Porsche, I will smash it to bits!*

His memory began filling in the blanks rapidly as he exited Maple Ridge, a real-estate stronghold for wealthy Tulsans, and location of only one of his (current) family's handful of homes.

Julie—she's a student. That's it. She goes to the University of Tulsa. Studying English, or anthropology, or something ridiculous like that.

He instinctively headed north, following Peoria Road for a little while, then took a right on Eleventh Street.

So she's probably headed there tonight. Going to the library, probably. She'll be able to tell me what happened the other night...which night was it?

Stek suddenly realized that he had absolutely no idea how long his "recovery" had lasted. Days? Weeks? A *month?*

Julie would know. And, after all, that fucking goblin had been banging on *her* door, so *someone* thought she was important.

STEVE WASN'T IN HIS room when Charley went to show him the map.

The isolation of the Place of Solace had finally started to get to Steve, who had taken to wanton acts of destruction—many of which were miraculously (and often to his dismay) reversed after a good night's sleep.

He had spray-painted his location on the door of Room 1.

MIRACLE ELIXIR ROCKS, DON'T IT?
MEET ME BACK AT THE GRAVEYARD.
GOT AN IDEA. *WAR!!!* – SC

The comment "WAR" was not an indication of his intentions. Steve thought it was funny to mess with hippies by saying "war" instead of "peace" as a closing salutation.

Charley grabbed fresh coffee and a sprinkled donut from the motel check-in and headed off to find out what Steve's idea was.

A strong breeze started when he was almost at the graveyard gate. Moonlight and streetlamps were enough to make the walk creepy, even if Charley felt reasonably sure (by this point) of his relative safety. Old mental habits die hard.

"*Chuck*!"

Charley practically leapt out of his skin at the sharp bark. Steve's laughter preceded him. Charley saw him shortly, jogging over and dodging tombstones.

"What's up, dude?" Charley said.

Breathlessly, Steve started talking.

"At first I thought we oughta just keep digging around that pipe, you know? Follow it one direction all the way, 'cause then we'd for sure hit something, even if it was just a sewage plant or whatever." They started walking back toward the pipeline they had discovered six feet below "Miller H. Life's" tombstone. "But then—*then*—I started thinking: why not just follow it with a metal detector, or something?"

They reached the brink of the hole.

"So I started figuring out the quickest way to get some souped-up metal detector that might be nearby, but when I got back here, in the quiet, I heard a sound." Steve pointed down at the pipe. "Listen."

Charley quieted himself and strained his ears. Suddenly, he heard it.

"A leak?" he suggested.

Steve grinned, nodding his head. "Yes! It's leaking! Check it out!"

Steve leapt into the hole and motioned for Charley to follow. Indeed, apparently due to some rough strike by one of their shovels, a tiny crack had appeared near a seam in the pipe.

Charley leaned in close and began to feel dizzy. "It's—woah," he commented.

"I *know*, dude!" Steve said. "Don't get too close, right? That shit's better than primo kief!"

"Don't you think we should talk to Roland about this?" he asked. He started feeling anxious again. "And just to confirm, you *did* leave a note under my door back at that motel, right?"

Steve looked perturbed. "No...I prefer spray paint," he said. "You found a note? That's fucking creepy. Roland, maybe? Can he do that without leaving the Emporium?"

Charley shrugged. "Don't know. I guess I'll ask him."

Steve turned his attention back to the pipe and pointed at it. "So we should probably head back to see if Roland's got the goods on this shit, huh?"

Charley nodded his head. "That, and see about my note."

"What does it say?" Steve asked as they took a rope ladder back out of the grave.

"It's a map," Charley answered.

Steve squatted at the edge of Miller's exhumation site and dusted off his hands. "A map, huh? Anything interesting?"

"It shows Mike Flowers's house. And something about a portal there?"

"No shit?" Steve said. He looked up at Charley. "The plot thickens."

He stood and pulled out his lighter and a cigarette.

"I'm not sure. I mean, there *was* something weird going on in the clubhouse, since that's where the box blew us up and landed us here."

Steve seemed preoccupied as they headed back to the cemetery gates.

"I think I need a few minutes to think about this. I'll meet you back at rendezvous." He trotted across the street beyond the gates and made a beeline for a Trans-Am parked outside of a quaint two-story house. Moments later, he was peeling out and waving.

The only other car Charley saw that was immediately available looked like it needed an oil change. And a headlight repair. And a windshield.

JULIE HAD MADE UP her mind. She was going to break in to McFarlin Tower and figure this goddamned thing out once and for all.

I'm paying rent to the "Garry" family, she thought to herself. *And I* know *it's the* Jarry *family from* Fear Club—*because*—*because*—*goddamn it,* I *don't know! But this is* far more *than fucking* coincidence*! Pete? And now this guy Stek shows up out of nowhere?* And *a shimmering light in McFarlin Tower?!?*

As for a plan?

That was precisely part of the test. She had already figured it out. She would push reality to the breaking point *tonight*— she would *force* that goddamned portal open; she'd kick, scream, break things, *burn the place to the fucking ground*—

She hesitated for a while in the parking lot of the library and checked her backpack. She'd thrown her copy of *Fear Club* in there, just in case, and a few more packs of cigarettes.

Pathetic, she thought. *Okay, so I can sneak in...maybe make it into the tower*—maybe. *But didn't they need that magic key for the elevator? Was* that *what made the portal appear?*

She got out of the car and decided to saunter along, just a regular student taking an evening stroll on campus. There were a few other kids around, a jogger, no security in sight.

Julie made it to one of the side entrances to the library in as unassuming a fashion as she could.

A figure, barely discernible from within the shadows to one side of the door, spoke.

"What's up, Julie?"

Julie froze briefly, then turned and attempted to sprint back through the patio.

"Wait!"

The voice sounded so earnest, so honest, she actually *did* stop and wait.

"It's Stek! Stek Jarry!" the figure announced, stepping into view with arms outstretched.

Julie *thought* she'd heard him say *Jarry* and not *Garry*...

"Jesus Christ, Stek!" Julie shouted. "You scared the shit out of me."

Stek shrugged. "Sorry," he said. "I didn't want you to do something stupid." He immediately cringed at the potential giveaway.

"Stupid? You *followed* me here?" she said, aghast.

"Well, yeah," he answered. "Like I said—"

"Why didn't you just *ask* to come with me?" she stated flatly, reaching into her denim jacket for a cigarette.

Stek's face broke into a grin and he chuckled briefly. "Shit," he said. "That's kind of a good question. I can see it from your perspective, you know? But let me tell you. The last time I worked *with* people, I ended up getting shot, then dumped into a lake, then I woke up, escaped, and got shot again. Speaking of which: you wouldn't happen to know *who*, exactly, shot me the other night?" He reached out a hand. "And perhaps more importantly: can I bum one of those?"

Julie sighed and handed him a Marlboro. Stek patted his pockets for a lighter, but Julie was quick with the Fabergé.

"Nice Zippo," Stek said.

"It's not a Zippo," Julie responded. "And no, I do *not* know who shot you a month ago," Julie said, then hesitated. "Or maybe I do. I don't fucking know."

"O-*kay*?" Stek responded. *What* did *this girl know?* "A month. Huh." He shrugged. "Hey, if you're trying to protect someone, that's cool—"

"I'm not," Julie said. "I'm just—are you?"

"Am I...?" Stek raised his eyebrows. Julie seemed to be having trouble getting something out.

Julie literally stamped her foot in frustration. Finally, when Stek grinned at her nervously, she spoke. "Are you going to explain yourself?"

"What?" Stek said.

Julie decided to go for broke. She *had*, after all, committed to acts of arson only moments ago for the sake of her wild hypothesis.

"What do you know about this place, Stek? About what's up there? In the Tower?"

Stek stood there silently for a moment, apparently trying to figure out how to explain *any* of what he wanted to say.

"Oh, yeah. Right. Yeah. There's kind of a—I don't know how to explain it. I guess I'll just—I don't know. Just tell you."

Julie crossed her arms and began glancing around. "Look, if you're not going to—"

Stek sighed. "I have my suspicions about all this, but—ah, well. Maybe one day it'll all come clear," he said.

"So—how about just coming out with it? I'm sure it's a mind-blowing, huge revelation," Julie said sarcastically.

Stek looked at her. *Why not?* "What the fuck, you know?" He took a drag off his cigarette. "There's a kind of gate. To another world. A portal. Up there in the Tower."

He paused momentarily. Julie didn't move or speak.

"To another *universe*," he emphasized, grinning nervously.

Julie stared at him. "You're *Stek Jarry*," she said. The world had suddenly collapsed into a pit of craziness where everything made sense.

Stek's grin widened. He spread his hands to either side. "Ta-da," he said. "Yeah, that's true. Not exactly the response I expected."

"No, I mean—" Julie pulled on her cigarette, flustered.

"Wait a minute," he said. "You *know* about this already—"

"I know about it," Julie said.

"Where in the—? How—?"

"I think that's where I'm from," she said. "The other place. *Golem Creek*."

Stek took a step back. He took another drag from his cigarette, then flicked it away.

"Huh," he said, crossing and uncrossing his arms. "Hm."

"Stek?" Julie said.

Stek looked up at the building, then back at Julie. "There are some bad people who know about this," he said. "Those guys who shot me—they—"

"I know all about it," Julie said, finally feeling the weight of *Fear Club* lifting from her. "Booker and Barton, or whatever. They shot you right after you got here. *You're from Golem Creek too.*"

Stek breathed out heavily. "Holy shit," he said. "You're fucking *Julie Evergreen.*" The realization began to dawn on him. "You know Charles Leland and—and, uh, whats-his-name—"

"Steve," Julie said. "Steve Chernowski."

A strong wind picked up, coupled with a sound like buzzing power lines.

"Julie," Stek Jarry said, "I think we've got to get out of here." He began to walk back in the direction of the parking lot, waving her along.

Julie followed hesitantly. What did she really know about this guy? *Fear Club* was pretty ambiguous about the Goblin Gang's motivations. What kind of person gets shot, anyway? And then dumped off...at their own *house*?

"And go where?" she asked. "And do what? This is just too fucking weird. Molly made me read that book—"

Stek froze. He turned to Julie and held her by the shoulders. "Molly Furnival made you read *what* book?" he asked, terror turning his eyes into saucers.

"*Fear Club,*" she said. "The book that Charley wrote. So she *is*—"

Stek was running to Julie's Honda.

"Wait up!" Julie yelled, frustration quickly outweighing apprehension. "What the hell? Where are you going?"

"*We* are going *back*!" he yelled over his shoulder. "We're going back to *Golem Creek*!"

CHAPTER TWO

THE WRITHING NUCLEAR CHAOS SHOW

AND THIS IS WHERE, dear reader, I pray that you will bear with me, your humble narrator, for I fear... I fear that... Ah, I suppose it will come clear shortly.

"Show, don't tell," is the protocol. Very well, then!

UPON ARRIVING AT THEIR destination, Charles Thomas Leland and Finnegan Stephanos Chernowski made a deeply disturbing discovery: the Dreamkeeper's Emporium was *gone*. In its place was a wooden "FOR SALE: 70 Prime Acres!" sign set into a field of dry weeds.

Nothing else had changed. But every sign of the Emporium had been, somehow, eradicated.

"Well," Steve said. "This is just a pile of 'fuck yous.' "

"How long were we *gone* for?" Charley asked, frantically casting his gaze about for some sign of the lost big fish.

"Not *that* long!" Steve said. He ran over to the sign and tried to pull it out of the ground. It wouldn't budge; a system of vines had coiled around its base, entangling it in the mystery of the altered landscape.

Charley frowned. "Okay, hang on a second," he said. "Are we sure that we're in the right *place*, first of all?"

Steve was still desperately trying to remove the sign from the field, as if getting rid of it would return the Emporium—a concept that, on reflection, seemed somehow more sane than it appeared on the surface, given their circumstances.

"Of *course* we're in the right fucking place, dude!" Steve

85

exclaimed, pausing in his altercation with the real estate sign for a moment. He pointed to several of the landmarks angrily. "Freeway. Strip mall. There's the fucking ice cream fountain!"

The ice cream fountain had been one of their favorite discoveries: an alabaster monument in the shape of a banana split set in the midst of what *would* be a large water-pond, if the latter wasn't being constantly refreshed with vanilla ice cream and various toppings from apertures in the sculpture.

Steve had, of course, been the first to taste it. Charley quickly followed. The event resulted in their very first sampling of one of Roland's miraculous elixirs—this one a green-tinted, black-licorice concoction, which Charley would forever after associate with the ability to sit up and breathe.

"Okay, all right," Charley said, unsure of what the hell *else* to say.

Steve stomped back over to him. "Not to mention the fucking *pyramid* is still right the hell there!" He angled an index finger at the looming edifice, silently resting in the midst of (and presumably *anchoring*) the Place of Solace.

"Is there—I don't know—some kind of *phone* we could use?" Charley asked wearily.

Steve's frown deepened. "You wanna *call* Roland?" he said, beginning to pace back and forth in front of him. "Sure, fine. Great idea. Oh, right—what the fuck's his number, again?"

Charley slumped to the ground.

"I guess we can hole up in one of those bed-and-breakfasts along the highway," Charley suggested. Steve began shaking his head.

"Or just hang out in a park nearby, or whatever," Charley continued. "Get a tent from a sporting goods store? I think I saw one a few blocks over. You know, keep watch? In case it comes back?"

Charley gazed up at Laban's pyramid. "Are we gonna have to—"

Steve shook his head and growled, having briefly shared Charley's apprehension regarding the monolith, hovering some twenty stories or more high. "*Hell* no, man! Last fucking resort! I ain't climbing that shit again." He continued to shake his head and utter barely intelligible imprecations against gods and men as he jogged over to the edge of the parking lot.

Charley thought back to the graveyard, to Miller H. Life, to the countless homes and shops and malls and parks and forests, et cetera, et cetera, et cetera, of the Place of Solace. *Where in the* world *would the Dreamkeeper's Emporium go? Why would it have disappeared* now? *Did it have something to do with the leaking pipe?*

About that moment, Steve shouted wildly and came sprinting back.

"Chuck! Can you believe it? I've got the *best* fucking idea *ever!*"

Charley managed a grin. Steve's "best ideas" typically landed him in the hospital. "Whaddaya got for me?"

"We *fly* up the pyramid!"

"*Fly?*" Charley responded. "Did you find an airplane or something? Do you know how to *pilot* an airplane?"

Steve shook his head, his smile ineradicable. "No way, dude! Better!" He began jogging away again. "Follow me! Check it out! *Magic carpet ride!*"

"*What?*" Charley managed, running after him. *This is, somehow,* not *going to turn out well, I can just* feel *it...*

"I THOUGHT THIS WOULD be more difficult," Charley said as he and Steve unlatched a big glass display case labeled AUTHENTIC FLYING CARPET.

Steve had managed to remember a place he'd been meaning to check out, a gigantic warehouse down the street—ARCADE GAMES OUTLET! Beside it squatted a weatherbeaten establishment that sold Persian rugs.

He was yanking the huge, heavy, rolled carpet out of its case. It looked to be about twenty feet wide—who knew how long it was. "This thing weighs a fucking *ton*," he observed. "And I thought there'd be some kind of alarm, or whatever."

The store itself was dark inside, illuminated by occasional little chandeliers and housed on its own in a two-story replica of a mosque surrounded by a moat of continually flowing golden waters. A library of thousands of Persian and Oriental rugs of all shapes and sizes and designs sprawled out within, covering walls and rolled up by the hundreds, leaning against paintings of various holy men. Here, a replica of Mohammed; there, a rendering of Zarathustra—even a strange oil painting of what appeared to be Jesus Christ as a dwarf.

"What makes you think this is going to work?" Charley asked. The find was unusual, but there *did* seem to be something about the Place of Solace in general that acceded to wishes, just like in dreams, where expectations grew into actual things and events.

Not necessarily always a variety that you *wanted*, but it beat fucking around for the time being.

Steve shrugged. "Worth a shot, I figure. Not to mention it would be fucking *awesome* if it *does* work."

"How did you even *think* of this—"

"*I Dream of Jeannie.*"

"What?"

"Back at that motel. *I Dream of Jeannie* reruns all fucking night."

"Ah, right," Charley said. He wondered if *The Munsters* reruns foreshadowed something, and, if so, what the hell *that* would be.

"Remember Prasad Veerma?" Charley asked. "He said this was how his uncle got opium into town."

Steve paused and looked at Charley over his shoulder. "Prasad Veerma? No shit?"

"No shit," Charley said. "You didn't know that?"

Steve shook his head and returned to wrenching the rug out of the glass case. Charley noticed dust puffing out of it— dust that disintegrated into sparkling lights that faded after a few seconds. He sneezed.

"Pete didn't dig any of that harder stuff," Steve explained. "I mean, he sometimes had it around. But that was just for personal—ah, personal—" He sneezed. "Use. Personal use."

Charley nodded. "Sure."

"How did you know about that?" Steve asked.

"Prasad told me," Charley said. There was finally enough room in the cramped aisle to help. The carpet, it turned out, did indeed weigh a fucking ton. "I guess he was high."

"Opium," Steve said aloud, musing as he waited for Charley to get a grip on one end of the rug. "To think that at one time I would've thought: 'Shit, I gotta get some of that! Waking dreams! How cool!' "

Charley laughed. "Now the only question is: 'How do I wake up?' "

YER OUTTA HERE! Soon enough, the main characters will die trying!

Charley winced. "Did you—uh, did you *hear*—"

Steve's mouth dropped open at the same time he dropped the rug.

"Um," Steve said. "So, uh, I'm thinking—" Steve suddenly raised his voice. "*Who the fuck*—"

"WHAT DID I EVER DO TO YOU?!?" God of Earth pleads insanity!

"And then he says something clever like that!" Steve said. "The bastard."

Charley backed away from the rug several steps. "Steve? Maybe we should just forget this idea, head back to the grave-yard, you know, maybe see if we can patch and re-bury the pipe? You think that would probably make the Emporium come back?"

CAVEAT! VACATE! This cat wants outta that bag!

Steve looked at me quizzically. I shook my head.

"C'mon, man," Steve said. "Come *on*! You gotta admit: you're curious, right? You wanna know just as much as *I* do, right?"

"Oh, sure, of course," Charley said. "This kind of thing *always* works out better than we plan it! Shit! Why not? I mean, whatever-it-is didn't just tell us we're going to *die trying* or anything, you know?"

Steve started laughing. "That's the spirit! Who the fuck ever said we were main characters? Help me get this weird sonofabitch into the parking lot."

Charley's reluctance disintegrated as they proceeded to maneuver the fuck-ton of rug out of the carpet store and into the parking lot beyond.

Outside, lightning flashed in a dark gray, swirling mass of clouds centered above them. An insistent breeze fluttered the store's canvas awnings and shook pink blossoms from a row of crabapple trees near the road.

"That's unusual," Charley said. "Have we ever seen a lightning storm here?"

Steve shook his head. He set his end of the carpet down on the asphalt. Charley followed suit. The scent of rain permeated the air.

"All right," Charley said. "What do we do now?"

"TOO MANY BIRTHDAYS!" yells oldest man in the world on his deathbed.

"What does that even *mean*?" Steve asked. "You want to help me unroll it?" He kicked one end of the rug. It barely budged.

HUSBAND FOUND DEAD AFTER CALLING WIFE A "COW": She cooked him into burgers and fed him to the dogs!

He frowned.

"I'll push this end while you get that one," Charley said. "Now I've *gotta* know what the hell is up."

IN FIVE MINUTES, THEY had the rug unfolded—all thirty feet of it.

"That wasn't so hard!" Steve said.

GET READY FOR IT! Major earth-shattering storm hits dream city!

And that's exactly what happened. A bolt of lightning struck the sky from the center of the unrolled rug, followed by a clap of thunder that shook buildings and ground alike.

Charley and Steve were thrust back in opposite directions by the force of it.

CLOWN CRISIS! Cotton candy shown to increase intelligence in carnival goers!

A second bolt of lightning, a second ear-shattering burst of thunder, and the biggest rain they'd ever witnessed in the "Place of Solace" had them drenched in seconds.

"*What do we do*?" Steve yelled through the din. Charley

could barely see him over on his side of the carpet—and that's basically what the rain was coming down like: carpets, not sheets.*

"*I don't know!*" Charley yelled back.

That's when he noticed smoke emanating from the rug's center.

Charley pointed at it frantically. "Check it out, dude!" he yelled. "It looks like it's burning!"

Steve sprinted over to Charley's side of the carpet. "This is just fucking *great*, man! One simple, basic fucking plan, and the thing's fucking ruined."

CAN YOU KNOW WHAT YOU HAVEN'T THOUGHT OF YET? Morons continue their blinding streak of idiocy through fabled land!

The black smoke grew thicker and began to spin, apparently unaffected by the downpour threatening to flood the parking lot and flush them out.

Rumbling thunder began again.

Steve suddenly turned to Charley. "That's not thunder!" he yelled.

Charley nodded slowly. "It's—it's fucking—"

Laughter. That's what it was. It was fucking *laughter.*

And the thing in the thickening black smoke suddenly took shape before them, as rain pounded the Place of Solace into submission.

"BACK AT THE RANCH," as they say, Wise Nerds waved before me, Roland, a thighbone.

"Not just any old femur!" Dr. Nerds insisted as he waved it back and forth.

I instinctively knew what he meant. No, really: I instinctively knew, as any Lama of Leng would.

He handed me the thighbone.

A sense of incalculable power flooded through me the instant my hand made contact with it. I felt simultaneously lighter than air and stronger than oak. Everything returned to me, revitalizing me like floodwaters

---

* Nice repeat of previously used metaphor, here. Very original.

permeating a desert.

Looking down, I discovered myself dressed in a most familiar uniform: dark robe, pointed cap, mala *beads wrapped about one wrist. The mass of tentacles descending from my face writhed in wonder as the realization of my extraordinary otherness hit home.*

"By the gods!" I exclaimed. (It seemed I was no longer speaking in my usual tongue.)

"Well, I suppose," Wise Nerds said, looking thoughtful. "In a sense, of course."

"Where have you been?" I asked.

Wise chuckled. "Nearly everywhere at once it seems! But I was just a moment ago in the Theatre d'Azif *with the Bhairavi Society. Talk about great popcorn!"*

My mind—clear and unobscured—immediately raced to Golem Creek, that peculiar linchpin of all the worlds I knew...

"I know what you're thinking!" Wise Nerds exclaimed.

I suddenly realized where we were.

"This is the—well, it's one of the graveyards in the—"

"Mittelwelt!"

"I always knew it as something else."

"Ah!" Wise Nerds scrabbled about the pile of remains he'd collected and extracted an unidentifiable relic. "It is also Its burial place."

Yassiz...

The name shook me like thunder.

I stated the obvious for confirmation. "We can traverse the worlds, then."

"Laban had you working at minimum capacity!" Wise responded. He paused in his labors and patted the front shirt pocket of his ubiquitous lab coat. "Some of us have mastered the process." He extracted a small gray pillbox and flipped it open. "No small thanks to my machinery."

I considered this as he grinned back at me and shook the contents of the pillbox into his mouth. His grin widened.

"I have internalized your machinery," I said.

"Indeed," Wise said after swallowing. "But I am still here!"

...that which remains...

Where did the worlds come from? I sat and gazed about, the sudden stark realization making its way over me like the moonlight over the gravestones.

"We're making this up," I said.

"From where?*" Wise asked, then began laughing. He checked his watch and his eyes goggled. "We've got to get back!"*

"But no time passes here!" I said.

"That doesn't matter!" Wise said, zipping up the duffel bag he'd filled with nameless parts. "We've alerted It." He held up the bag as some degree of explanation.

I sighed, abiding in unencumbered zhiné *and faultless, shimmering* rigpa *for a few "moments."*

Wise continued speaking. "Okay, when you get back, it'll be a little foggy at first—er, the computation might take a little while to reconfigure what you're used to—but don't worry! You should be—oh, wait—hang on, shouldn't be any trouble—ah, okay, didn't quite *expect that—"*

IN FRONT OF THEM—RAIN, thunder, and lightning still hammering down and sky black as night—stood a ten-foot tall, tentacled monstrosity.

For the most part, at least. The thing changed shape like a balloon of hovering, hot mercury, as did the lightning flashing and streaking and crawling through and across the sky. These two phenomena may or may not have been related, just as the thing's extraordinary laughter may or may not have been related to the rumbling, chuckling thunder which appeared to echo it.

"My oppression—is *ended*!" Its laughter could fill the voids between planets, and shook both Charley and Steve like toy train cars handled by mad, scheming five-year-olds.

Charley glanced at Steve, whose eyes were riveted to the entity before them. It had now sprouted a pair of enormous bat-like wings which flapped uninhibitedly in the storm, causing small mini-tornadoes of rain. As the wings continued to beat, eyes like hot coals gazed into them from the cloak of night forming its indeterminate body. The storm began to diminish somewhat, although it continued to rain, thundering and casting flickers of lightning periodically.

Steve nudged Charley. "Ask it what it is!" he whispered harshly.

The thing heard Steve's request clearly. "You may call me

Roland!" it thundered. "I am the *Dreamkeeper!*"

DON'T BELIEVE EVERYTHING YOU SEE! Teenage grandmother confesses to use of time machine!

"Roland?" Charley said aloud inadvertently.*

"Shit," Steve lamented. "Shit, shit, *shit!* This just ain't right."

Charley turned to Steve. "What do we do now?" he said. "I mean, you heard that, right?"

"As payment to those who released me," the phantasm calling itself "Roland" continued, "I grant the customary three wishes."

Steve was suddenly all ears. "Now *that's* an offer!" he immediately asserted, expressing far too little hesitation. "Three wishes!" He jerked his thumb toward Charley. "So what does *he* get?"

Charley gave Steve a sarcastic smile. "Very funny," he said.

"Three wishes to those responsible for my release! Ask, and it is yours," the wavering Roland-Warp continued.

"Well, that wasn't much of an explanation," Charley said to Steve. "Doesn't divide evenly, I mean."

"This is super-easy," Steve said. Charley immediately cringed and patted himself reflexively, lamenting the lack of duct tape to silence him with. "We just wish for—"

Charley clamped the palm of one hand over Steve's mouth and raised his other hand in a fist. "*No!*" he yelled. "Not yet! *Wait!*"

Steve mumbled, eyes wide, for a moment, then nodded. Charley slowly released him, keeping his fist raised threateningly.

"All *right,*" Steve said. "All right!" He turned back to the creature, which hovered just above the "flying carpet" with its arms crossed. "Look, monster-thing, Roland, whatever! What the hell happened to the Emporium? And if you're

---

* I can at least still insert annotations! I had a *feeling* something like this was going to happen! Sorry, trying to get through to Steve and Charley seems to be causing some feedback-loop problems. Maybe the signal's traveling through commercials hovering in the void on old radio waves? I'm going to figure it out—hang on—

really *Roland*, then why aren't you, I don't know—shorter? You know. And wearing glasses?"

"Nice one, Stevie," Charley said.

"Shorter?" Roland said, flickering. "I can be...shorter... Do you wish for this?"

"*No!*" Charley shouted as Steve began to nod. "No! Not at all. We do *not* wish for that!" He gave Steve a furious look. Steve shrugged.

"Um, okay," Charley said. "We're just wondering—we're not *wishing* anything, okay, we're just *wondering*—uh, could you, maybe, I don't know—"

"Tell us about that weird pipeline we dug up out in yonder graveyard?" Steve finished for him.

Instantly, they were sitting beside each other, dry and warm, in a booth at a Waffle House—*sans* waitresses, patrons, and, thankfully, jukebox music. But a Waffle House nonetheless.

Roland (looking exactly like his old self again, save for a name tag which read "HELLO! MY NAME IS: ???") sat across from them. "You *found* that?"

Steve uttered a cry of exasperation. "Roland! What the fuck? What was all that shit about?"

Roland grinned and stirred the coffee that had suddenly appeared before him. "Oops. Big show. Don't worry about it."

"Don't *worry* about it?" Charley shouted. "Jesus Christ, dude! Did you get *bored* or something without us around?"

Roland shrugged. "I guess. Like I said—sorry."

"Does this have to do with us cracking that pipe?" Charley asked.

"Oh, *man*. The *pipeline*." Roland grinned and leaned back in the booth. "What a *find*! That's how Laban gets the magic in."

Steve and Charley looked at each other.

"The magic?" Steve said.

Roland nodded. "Or *mana*. Or *æthyr*. Or whatever you want to call raw dream-stuff before it's molded by thought and intention."

"He just pipes the shit in!" Steve said, astonished.

"Where does he get it?" Charley asked. "What's the

source?"

Roland shrugged. "Fuck if I know," he said with unchar-acteristic fervor. He began jerking his head back and forth nervously. "Where's the bathroom?" he said loudly before practically falling out of his seat and running to the other end of the diner.

"I think we should lay off that question," Charley said once Roland had closed the bathroom door behind him.

"No shit. He sounds like he's half drunk. Has that guy *ever* gone to the bathroom before?"

Charley shook his head. "Maybe that's one of those fail-safe things? I mean, what if he just blows up or something when he's pressured into revealing some major secret?"

Steve nodded and lit a cigarette. "We'll change the subject when he gets back. Maybe ask him about those wishes, right?"

Charley had time to take a single, seemingly eternal sip of his terrible, cold coffee before Roland came bouncing back, apparently his usual chipper self.

"So is that what you really look like?" Steve asked as soon as Roland sat down. "An old-school genie, or whatever?"

"Maybe," Roland replied cryptically. He took a sip of his coffee. "This is exceptional."

Charley grimaced.

"So...how would you know?" Steve asked.

"Know what?"

"That you're a genie?"

"Are you crazy?"

"Yes, he's crazy," Charley answered. "What a weird-ass question, dude." Steve turned to Charley and mouthed—silently and all-too-obviously—the words: *I want my three wishes!*

Roland pointed at a spot on the table. "What's that?" he asked.

"What's what?" Steve responded.

"That! *That*! Right there!"

"I don't *know*!" Steve shouted, looking from the table to Charley to Roland and back to the seemingly empty spot. "What? A table?"

Instantly, a miniature version of their table appeared, *on* the table, sporting action-figure versions of each of them.

"Woah! That's slick," Steve said, hesitantly reaching out for the Steve-Figure.

"Oh," Charley said. "So, you're kind of like magic *first*, reality second?"

Roland shrugged and nodded.

Steve frowned as he lifted up the doll. "I thought I might go flying into the air if I did that," he admitted. He sighed and set the remarkably accurate figure down. "So, let's say, if that mini-table was *actually* a triple-decker bacon cheeseburger from Lots-a-Burger—"

Suddenly, all three sat at an ornate oak table beset with a silver platter, on which lay any fast-food addict's five-star cuisine.

Steve's frown became a grin. He reached over and picked up the burger. Roland nodded. Steve looked at Charley once, then shrugged and took a huge bite.

His eyes closed. As he chewed, tears began to well up and roll down his cheeks. "It's—*perfect*," he finally said. He paused to sniffle, then took another bite, before suddenly, anxiously asking, "We're not using up our three wishes, are we?"

Roland shook his head, grinning amiably.

"What's the catch, though?" Charley said, eyeing the burger. "I mean, you can just create and destroy at will? No catch?"

Roland smiled. A second course appeared on the table, and a huge plate of steak fries with bowls of ketchup and mayonnaise (Steve's favorite condiment) suddenly lay between them. Two throne-like chairs were now on either side of the table. Roland looked at Charley and gestured to the meal.

"The 'catch,' if you will," Roland explained as Steve and Charley ate, half-listening, "is *concentration*. Moments ago, this was not here; moments from now, it will be no more. Such is the way of all phenomena. As we need it to be, in the sense of its existence as a necessary aspect of our context, so it is. Then?" He waved a hand.

Instantly, Steve and Charley were at Lots-a-Burger during a hopping Friday night. The table and chairs had become an outdoor bench near the back of the establishment. Roland sat on Steve's side of the aluminum table, eating steak fries. Carloads of Honorius High teenagers cavorted and shouted, screamed and jumped, played music and made out and broke up and raised general hell—like any other Friday night at the Lots-a-Burger. A week's worth of pent-up energy fueled and focused the fires of what would otherwise be your usual displaced aggression, with only one oddity: many of them were in Halloween costumes.

Steve's eyes were still closed as he savored the remainder of the triple-decker bacon cheeseburger, one of the multiverse's finest inventions. Charley's eyes went wide.

"We're back," Charley spoke hoarsely. "We're fucking *back*!"

Steve opened his eyes slowly, his mind still reeling from food-induced theta waves.

Suddenly, he stood, eyes now wide with shock. He shoved the last bite of the cheeseburger in his mouth, then leapt onto the table.

"*Fuuuuuck YEEEEEAH!*" he shouted. Charley bounced out of his seat, uncontrollably smiling, and hooted into the night air.

Steve jumped off the table and ran up to a nerdy-looking girl in a witch's hat fumbling with the lock of her car door. "What's going on, honey?" he asked, grinning, and grabbed her by the hips in an attempt to do a dance move.

She slapped him. Its audibility made Charley wince, but in no way dampened Steve's spirits.

"Hey! Just trying to share the magic, you know—" Steve flung his hands into the air.

The girl had extracted pepper spray from her purse.

As Steve spun away from her, the howling started.

Then the screams.

"Uh, Steve?" Charley said, glancing around frantically.

"Shit!" Steve said. "It was just a joke, you know?" He then met Charley's gaze and paused. The girl gave up the attack and leapt into her car.

"Oh, fuck," he said. The howling increased in volume,

a demonic chorus surrounding them. Cars started, tires screeched, and chaotic shouting and more screams bled through their common realization as customers began fleeing like uncaged rodents.

"Where's Roland?" Charley asked. He grabbed Steve by the shoulders and shook him. "Where the *fuck* did he go?"

CHAPTER THREE

MAKE ROOM FOR
IAK SAKKAK

THE HONORIUS HIGH MONSTER Ball had grown to a monster-sized mash of frightening proportions over the years. No one quite remembered the tradition's origins, but, much like a graveyard, it just seemed to keep getting larger and more inhabited. The Monster Ball Committee went out of their way to make each "Halloween II" an even bigger Halloween celebration than All Hallows' Eve Itself. Black and orange banners lit with thousands of orange Christmas-style lights hung over and around every window and door. Most of the halls had the usual fluorescent lighting replaced with ultra-violet, to illuminate the Halloween II Art Committee's eerie paintings and decorations.

Images, sculptures, statues, and carvings of imps and demons, goblins and ghouls, werewolves and vampires and mummies lurked, prowled, skulked, and lay in wait throughout Honorius High. As the first waves of costumed teenagers began flooding in, Mrs. Blair Trundle of the Music Department ensured that the speaker system piped nothing but spooky sounds of creaking doors, yowling cats, howling wolves, and various screams and shrieks.

It was a true temple of the *qliphoth*, the vestiges of forgotten potencies, repressed and relabeled demonic. It was a dark, haunted, hellmouth made flagrant and unapologetic. It was the Enemy Incarnate, flocking with emissaries of evil.

It was high school.

And now, on Walpurgisnacht, as a vast Egg Moon rose in

the east, as The Borgo Pass tuned their guitars and tightened their drumheads backstage, it yawned in welcome to Golem Creek's sinister brood...

WESTON GRAY *FELT THE* arrival of the two young men in Golem Creek—it was the psychic-emotional equivalent of tearing fabric or cracking a plank of wood.

"They're *here*," he had said aloud to Yassiz, not understanding what the spontaneous pronouncement implied.

Yassiz had grinned with that supremely infernal look of *knowing* he could whip about like a throwing knife. "Then the game's almost up," he'd said mysteriously, disappearing into the shadows of the sub-basement in the Flowers house on Brake Street.

"What am I supposed to—" Weston began.

But Yassiz was gone.

Something had changed.

He gazed at the room about him, lit by the flickering lights of sconces on the walls. *The circle was complete.*

Its beauty smacked of mass graves and the catastrophic darkness of unplumbable depths. Specific bones of the girls he'd fed to Yassiz had each been painstakingly cleaned, each one lovingly assembled in its proper place in the mandala within which Weston now stood. The vertebrae and ribs outlined sigils Yassiz had led Weston in the construction of; three skullcaps fitted with three precisely molded bowls of *electrum magicum* now shimmered with pools of magically lique-fied antimony at their centers.

Weston shook a handful of Tom Fallow's Valentine's Day hearts—one of their unnameable purposes fathomed at last—from a dark velvet bag into a mortar and began to grind them. A murmuring, insectile chant emanated from the gran-ules' braying.

"*Ia...Ia...Yog Sothoth! Ia...Ia...Nyarlathotep! Veni, Nyarlathotep... Veni!*"

The glittering dust gave off small bursts of light that took shape briefly before disintegrating like hypnagogic imagery against the room's shadowy walls. Weston portioned out a third of the dust into each of the skullcaps.

An invigorating, electrical hum erupted from everywhere and nowhere as the liquid in the first skullcap began vibrating and glowing with a hot orange light. The hum and the light intensified as Weston added the dust to each of the two remaining skullcaps.

"*Ol sonuf vaoresagi...*" Weston began the formal invocation as he carefully poured the contents of each of the skullcaps into a small silver cauldron. The electrical hum became an unbearable din as the last of the liquid was intermixed, finally climaxing in a burst of rainbow light that shot from the cauldron through the roof of the chamber, blowing Weston backwards.

Then, blackness...*blackness, and a sound like millions of cackling, groaning, wailing, howling voices...rounding them all up, heading off to the show...*

THE LOTS-A-BURGER CLEARED OUT in record time. Even Skimp Buckles (a manager notorious for his miserly attitude—hence the moniker) peeled out in his Ford Festiva, trusting the hysteria of the crowd to keep him safe from whatever terrors had assaulted them.

Howling followed the crowds of fleeing patrons. Charley had been certain he'd caught a glimpse of dark shapes moving with incredible speed through the shadows of the back parking lot, and grabbed hold of Steve. They ducked into a nook beside one of the Lots-a-Burger dumpsters.

Other than the standard pungent scent of dumpster-cocktail, they met nothing untoward. The howling and chaos diminished, heading in the direction of Honorius. In short order, they were alone in the littered parking lot.

"Dude!" Steve exclaimed, extracting himself from beside the dumpster. "They *absquatulate*! Holy *longshanks*!"

"What *was* it?" Charley asked. "And where the fuck is Roland?"

Steve shook his head, smiling. "Don't know, man," he said. "All I know is, we ain't banned in G.C. no more!" He started laughing.

Charley swung his gaze over the Lots-a-Burger, still buzzing with light and the soft sound of WOTO playing modern pop hits over the staticky intercom system.

Golem Creek. There it was again, around him, just like that. As easy as anything. *That goddamned genie*—

"That goddamned genie could've sent us back here *any time*?" Charley shouted.

Steve nodded. "Looks like it," he said, trotting up to the Lots-a-Burger door and pulling on the handle. "Rats! Locked."

"Jesus," Charley said. He slumped down on one of the benches in front of the drive-in parking places. "So what the hell was he waiting for?"

"Tonight, I guess," Steve said. His eyes brightened as he surveyed the parking lot.

"Okay, great, we're back in Golem Creek," Charley said. "Now what? Find Julie? Go home and go to sleep? I mean, we've been in fucking dreamland for—Christ, how long now? And we're supposed to just walk right the fuck back in and start—what? Going to school, again?"

Steve's enthusiasm waned slightly. "No shit," he said, pulling on the locked door handle of what appeared to be an abandoned brown Camaro. "I just realized we're going to have to start paying money for things again."

Charley groaned. "All that time! All that time in the Place of Solace. There has to be something more to all this. What does it mean? Why did he bring us back *now*? Is it some kind of weird punishment for springing a leak in Laban's magical plumbing system?"

Charley stood up. "Look," he said, "I say we head over to Julie's. Find out if she's there."

"Why was everybody wearing costumes?" Steve asked.

Charley shook his head. "I have no idea," he said. "Let's at least start moving."

Charley headed toward the sidewalk in front of the Lots-a-Burger. He heard Steve jogging up behind him. They were on Yates Street. They could go south and get to Julie's—and, by the gods, he could check in with his parents... He didn't want to think about that. *How long had he been gone?*

Chicken Hill loomed eerily in the light of a full moon in the distance.

"This is insane," Charley said. "Too warm for Halloween—"

"It's the Monster Ball!" Steve shouted, perking up again. "It's the night of the fucking Monster Ball!"

"So we didn't get back around the same time we were last in Golem Creek?" Charley asked.

Steve shrugged. "Guess not. You wanna go check it out? I mean, get Julie, then go check it out?"

Charley shrugged. "If Roland's going to just abandon us like that, without any explanation," he said, "I guess we can't go wrong." As if on cue, spine-tingling howls began again, this time clearly discernible from the direction of Honorius High.

"Whaddaya know?" Steve said, pointing. "Fate wants us there."

"How do we know this isn't just some weird dream-overlap thing?" Charley asked.

Steve shrugged. "Should we get a cab?" he suggested. Charley shook his head. "No. Right. But if it *was* a dream-overlap thing, then—wait. Roland wouldn't have disappeared, right? I mean, he can exist in the overlap part of the worlds, can't he?"

Charley shook his head again. "I have no idea."

"We act like it's the place we've got to be, then, I guess," Steve said. "Hey, wouldn't it be cool if everything worked out perfectly, like when you expect everything to go right in a dream?"

Car headlights appeared around a corner in the distance. Steve and Charley looked at each other.

"That's reassuring," Charley said, frowning.

"I'm going to flag it down," Steve said.

"No, don't—" Charley started. Steve had already sprinted ahead, waving his arms.

The car approached, a nondescript black sedan.

"Hey!" Steve shouted. "Yo! Dude!"

The car slowed. Steve ran to the driver's window, which had rolled down.

"You think you could give us a ride?" Steve asked. "To South Street? Or Honorius, if you're going the other direction?"

Weston Gray nodded. "I'm headed to the Monster Ball," he said in a monotone. "Are you and your friend in trouble?"

HE DID INTRODUCE HIMSELF as Weston Gray, but only several awkward beats after Charley and Steve had introduced themselves, as if he'd forgotten standard communication procedure.

The ensuing silence was somehow more terrifying than if the weirdo had been playing Muzak or even, gods-be-damned, smooth jazz. Steve, from his tense position in the front seat, occasionally cast a glance back at Charley, as if to assure himself that they were both still there, or that Roland wasn't playing some sort of mean trick on them.

"So, uh," Charley said, more to relieve Steve's obvious tension than anything else. "You new at Honorius?"

Weston, not taking his eyes off the road, said, "Kind of."

"Hm," Charley responded. Steve glanced back again, then forward, then appeared to give up and started gazing out the window.

"Crazy howling noises," Charley said. "I wonder what's going on."

"Prank, probably," Weston said. He extracted a black Nat Sherman and depressed the cigarette lighter.

Steve suddenly perked up. "Woah!" he said. "Haven't seen one of those in a while!"

"Right," Weston said without offering him one. "I'm sorry. I'm a little distracted tonight." It seemed to take him some effort to make this explanation.

He waited for the lighter to pop out, then lit his cigarette. Steve shrugged, pulled out a Camel Wide, and lit it with a Bic.

Charley decided that further attempts at communication would be futile.

"I need to stop for gas," Weston said flatly as they

approached a FazMart about a block away from Honorius.

"Hey, that's cool," Steve said, inadvertently opening his door a crack before they'd even rolled to a stop in front of the gas pumps. "We can walk the rest of the way." He hopped out of the car and bowed, opening Charley's door for him.

Charley was frozen in the back seat.

"Chuck?" Steve said uncertainly.

Weston stepped out of the car and took out his wallet. He had ceased paying any attention to them.

Steve peered into the shadows of the back seat. "Chuckie? You want to *walk* the rest of the *way*?" he urged, motioning strongly with both arms and silently mouthing, *This dude's CRAZY!*

Charley shivered noticeably, then slid out of the seat and closed the door. Weston had already walked into the FazMart. They could see him handing the clerk cash.

They were half a block away before Charley let out a loud, gasping breath.

"Holy fuck!" he shouted hoarsely.

"What!" Steve grabbed one of his shoulders and shook it. "What the fuck happened back there, dude?"

"That guy wasn't human," Charley said.

"Well, yeah, no shit," Steve said. "That was kind of obvious, wasn't—"

"No! No. I mean he was *not* a human being."

Steve stopped walking. "Wait a minute," he said.

"Yeah! Yes!" Charley said. They had reached the parking lot of Bang for Your Buck Liquor, which lay just within reach of Honorius High School. The owner had fought and won a lawsuit against the city claiming that it violated a zoning restriction for liquor stores within sight of public schools. Everyone knew that the football field expansion following the lawsuit—and the continued existence of Bang for Your Buck—had been a settlement deal.

A few kids stood around, waiting to see if one of the patrons would buy them alcohol.

"When we passed through that patch of moonlight just before the FazMart, I saw his reflection in the rear-view mirror," Charley explained. "And it was—it was like—like one of those things from the Murk, almost."

"Well," Steve said, nodding at a cute blonde next to a payphone, costumed as some sort of disco girl. She fluffed her already dramatically large pigtails and ignored him. "That settles it."

"Settles what?" Charley asked. "There are *monsters* here in human form—"

"*Trust no one*," Steve said. He grinned at the blonde, who glanced briefly at him, then turned to her friend and started speaking to her rapidly.

"Great advice," Charley said. "I think we were kind of already doing that."

Steve gazed wistfully at the glass door of Bang for Your Buck and burst out laughing.

"What the fuck?" Charley said.

Steve snorted. "Shit, man, I can't believe this," he said, chuckling. "Hey, I've got a plan, all right? Just—just follow along, all right? I just remembered something."

"You mean you want me to trust you?" Charley asked. "Because you just told me not to do that."

"Just play along, all right?" Steve insisted, smiling widely. He patted Charley on the shoulder. "Hang on one sec," he said, and strode rapidly over to the disco girl. Charley watched in amazement.

"Excuse me!" he shouted at her. She looked from side to side for some form of escape. "Pardon me, ma'am!"

"What do *you* want?" she asked in a huff.

"I was just wondering if you could tell me something."

The girl stared straight at him. Her friend, an inexpertly done-up Vampirella, appeared to be looking for a convenient way to flee the scene. "Well?" she said, adjusting a sequined purse strap over one shoulder of her shiny, multicolored jacket. "What is it?"

"Do you know me?" Steve asked.

"What the hell is that supposed to mean?"

"It's a simple question," Steve responded. "Do you know who I am?"

"Of course I know who you are," she said. "And if you're trying to pull some clever stunt with me, it's not going to work."

Steve laughed. "C'mon, Jessica, it's not like that—"

"You stood me up!" the girl—Jessica, apparently—shouted, stomping one high-heeled boot in defiance.

"You have *got* to understand something here!" Steve said. "I was transported to another world, where—"

"Oh, give me a break!" Jessica said, turning back to her friend. "Let's get out of here."

"Wait!" Steve said, still smiling uncontrollably, but seeming suddenly desperate. "Hang on. Don't hold a grudge! You want booze? I can get you booze!"

Jessica stopped and turned back to him. "I don't want any of that Mad Dog shit you got last time—"

"Nah, nah! No way! Only the finest Bacardi for my dancin' queen!"

Jessica forced an inadvertent grin back to a frown. "Stephen! Get me alcohol!"

"All right! No prob," Steve said. He yelled over his shoulder. "Yo, Chuckie! Could you get these ladies some refreshments while I explain myself?" Turning back to Jessica, he said, "He's twenty-one. Seriously! So, who's your friend?"

Charley shook his head, astonished, unwilling to play along yet unable to find a good reason not to. How the hell did he know that girl? Charley didn't remember ever seeing her before...though something about her seemed familiar...he just couldn't quite figure it out...

He headed for the doors of Bang for Your Buck. *What the hell is Steve's plan? It's not like I've got any cash—*

Roland sat behind the register, watching the news on a little black-and-white television sitting on the counter. "Evenin'!" he said as Charley walked into the store. "Help you find something?"

"WHAT IS YOUR *DEAL*, man?" Charley whispered fiercely, leaning across the counter.

"Hey, it's cool, man!" Roland said. "Check it out. Werewolf

attack!" He gestured to the little television set.

"*...authorities are on the scene now. No casualties have been reported, and although the purported attack appears to be a Monster Ball-related act of mischief, Sheriff Rigley intends to treat the disturbance as an actual threat until further notice...*"

"Cool, huh?" Roland laughed.

"What the fuck is going on?" Charley said. "Where are we?"

"Golem Creek, man," Roland said. "Obviously. Hey, move over one sec."

A tall, thin blond guy wearing a black trench coat stepped up to the cash register with a fifth of Jim Beam.

"Big night ahead, eh, Tom?" Roland commented, chuckling.

"Tell me about it," Tom Fallow said. "Talk about busy!"

They both started laughing. Tom handed him a twenty-dollar bill and said, "Keep the change."

"Much obliged!" Roland responded. "Not much more to do! Hang in there!"

Charley watched the exchange, astonished. As Tom stepped out of the store, he heard Steve launch into his "Shaggy & Scooby Die" routine.

At least the girls would be entertained.

Charley shifted back in front of the counter. "Seriously, Roland, c'mon! You've got to fess up. What are we supposed to be doing here? And if you could get us here the whole time, why did you wait so long?"

"Everyone had to be in place," he said, grinning. "It will all turn out the way it needs to! You'll start noticing memories returning, just like last time you skipped out on reality." He chuckled. "The longer you stick around, the more natural it will feel. You know how it works! Experience of a thing provides its own reasons for being there, here and now— whether or not it 'actually' happened."

Charley was speechless. He glanced around the store. Customers milled about in their own little worlds, totally unaware of how literal that metaphor was.

Roland held a bottle of Bacardi 151 which had appeared

from out of nowhere. "Don't worry about a thing! Go! Enjoy yourself. The show's about to start! Isn't it great? The wait's over!" He shoved the Bacardi into a paper bag.

Charley noticed his heart rate increase. He breathed heavily. "What the—" he attempted to remain calm, and failed. "What the fuck are you getting at?"

Roland handed him the bag. "Your drink, sir, on the house," he said calmly, still grinning. "For the ladies. Can't upset the ladies. Not tonight."

Charley took the bag. His shoulders slumped. "Fine," he said. "Fine! Not a straight answer. Not one straight fucking answer. All I wanted." He looked up at Roland. "Go to hell."

Roland leaned back on his stool and started chuckling in response. Charley backed away from the counter. Laughter followed him out the door, into the parking lot, where Jessica and her friend had forgotten themselves, doubled over with more laughter, and Steve/Shaggy wrestled with himself, trying to get the gun out of Steve/Scooby's hands, pleading with Shaggy's voice *not to do it, don't do it, Scoob!*

THE DEVIL STOOD IN their midst, bands of seminude witches flocking about Him, grave evil in myriad scabrous forms slithering over worm-ridden earth beneath. Above, in a villainous carapace of black sky, gibbous yellow Hecate's Eye unblinking and attendant, haloed in ghastly, glowing green, giving way to the Mouth of Hell, the wide, fangéd jaws of Belial or Leviathan—Claxton Christopher wasn't quite sure if it mattered which, frankly.

He considered it his crowning achievement, his personal Ghent Altarpiece: the Honorius High Monster Ball Mural, draped in heavy faux silk over the entrance to the school, through which hordes of creatures and capering carousers flocked, brimming over with lust and mirth and too much pre-dance vodka.

Clax sat on the little hill overlooking the parking lot and took out his annual doobie. Pete Jarry made it special for him, once a year: a grand mixture of *Cannabis sativa* marinated according to "an ancient formula of the Druids" (Pete always said with a laugh) in sweetened shroom-juice.

Now was the time to rest, reflect, and, ultimately, fall upstairs. Clax basked in the moon's glow and took out his pipe lighter. Seconds later, the first pangs of dread marking the onset of waking dream accelerated through him. He became suddenly aware of deep bass from The Borgo Pass as they strummed out the beginning of "Rock 'n' Roll High School" by The Ramones, just like they always did, the ritual repeated, year after year...

His mind wandered, drifting in and out of the susurrant, chattering multitudes swarming about the parking lot, re-con-stituting their goblinry after making out in dark cars or behind the bleachers around back, chugging sixers of cheap beer and laughing and belching around running clown makeup, sneaking tokes and smokes of all varieties before slinking into the Belly of the Beast.

He smiled. He watched the flickering moon above, as vast and glimmering as the one in his painting. Dark shapes began swimming about in the sky. *Kicking in FAST this time! All* right...

"Good stuff. I can tell."

The voice spoke from somewhere behind or above him, and he started, slightly.

"Right?" Clax said. It wasn't what he'd intended to say, but it worked.

"Mind if I join you?"

Clax watched as the dark shape became a person who dropped to the earth beside him with a shuddering crash. (That was the smoke. For sure.)

"Name's Nashe," the figure said. "I've come to watch the fallout."

"Clax," managed the slumped and grinning artist. "My name. Is."

"Right on, dude," Nashe said, and pulled a flask from the inner pocket of his leather jacket. "This is going to be incred-ible, isn't it? *Car l'amour et la mort n'est qu'une même chose.*"*

---

* "Because love and death are the same thing." Ronsard, *Le Second livre des*

Clax managed a nod, then started laughing.

"Careful," Nashe said, nodding to the mega-joint in Clax's hand. "You don't want to lose that."

"Hell no!" Clax said, and noticed himself sitting back up, feeling suddenly more alert.

"Cheers," Nashe said, grinning, and tipped the flask toward Clax before drinking from it. "*Comburite libros.*"*

Clax nodded and smiled, not giving much of a fuck. Both of them turned to face Honorius High. Clax took another deep drag before producing clouds of bluish smoke that seemed to wash over the unsuspecting partygoers' heads.

"I PROMISE YOU THAT is *exactly* the place!"

Stek Jarry's urgency had ramped up considerably. Julie felt a bit cornered by the sudden rush of revelations. They were racing down Sheridan Road now, toward the other end of town entirely. She noticed that she was speeding, absorbing the pressure of his anxiety and allowing it to influence her.

"Look, dude, I'm aware that everything you're telling me is—" Julie stopped herself. What was it, after all? Convincing? Bullshit? Likely? Unlikely?

"It's our only chance of getting back," Stek insisted. "That portal is in the basement! Or, what *was* the basement."

"What about the one in McFarlin Tower?" Julie asked. They whizzed past a QuikTrip parking lot full of cops. She let off the gas and hoped they'd gone unnoticed.

Stek was jumping up and down in his seat. "It's a trap! I told you. That's the one that leads into Laban's tomb! It's been—compromised."

"I'm still not sure you didn't just read the same damned book as me," Julie said, checking her rear-view mirror. None of the cops seemed to be following, thank the gods.

"I'm *in* the damned book!" he reminded her. "You *know* that! Pete, me, Charley, Steve, *you*—we're *all* in the goddamned book!"

---

sonnets pour Hélène, LXXIX.
* "Burn your books." Severinus, *Idea medicinæ*, 73.

"And Molly," Julie said. "Don't forget Molly."

Stek groaned. "Trust me," he said. "I'm not about to forget Molly-fucking-Furnival."

"What is the deal with you two, anyway?" Julie said. *This is it,* she thought. *This is where I jump in the loony bin with the crazy guy, and start believing his story, hook, line, and sinker...even if it* is *mostly true...*

"We've got sort of a—what would you call it? A hate-hate relationship?" he said.

"You mean that you dated and broke up?" Julie suggested.

"Yeah, sort of," Stek said. "Kind of."

"Listen, dude, I suggest you get much better at your bull-shitting if you want to keep me convinced. We're driving out to an abandoned, burned-down estate in the fucking boon-docks. And keep in mind that I will fucking *cut* you if you so much as *look* at me weird when we get out there." Julie slowed for a red light. They were at the bottom of the hill where 71st Street crossed Sheridan. The mundane glow of the twenty-four hour Reasor's grocery store on the corner made an eerie contrast with her wildly inadequate grasp of the situation at hand.

She knew she was being unreasonable, given the context. Something within her kept wanting to pull her *back* to *this* world...as if being "in the world" was ruled by the same sort of inertia as falling objects. Julie pulled out a Marlboro and lit it. Stek was silent for a moment.

"*Cut* you, motherfucker," she repeated, deciding that she ought nonetheless try to maintain some degree of control over the veritable stranger in her car. "Won't even think twice about it. Let you bleed out and forget this ever happened."

Stek sighed. "I'm sorry," he said. "I'm a little out of it. I think the painkillers are wearing off, too. Fuck." He pressed a palm gingerly to his left side. The newly healed scar where the last bullet had passed through him felt warm to the touch. *Probably infected or something*, he thought. *Great.*

Julie tried to focus on her cigarette and the "facts." The light turned green and they proceeded through it.

"Okay," she said. "All right. It's weird. Everything's *too* weird. It's actually just weird enough to all be true." As if confirming her suspicions, an identical 1981 Honda Civic with two passengers in it drove past them, going the other direction. *Probably us, for Christ's sake, in some other goddamned time stream, or whatever...*

"I can tell you this much," Stek said. "I'll tell you straight. Since you already only half believe me"—Julie glanced over at him and arched an eyebrow—"or *don't* believe me yet, I might as well lay it all out for you." Stek heaved a sigh. "I think a lot of this might be my fault."

"No shit?" Julie laughed.

"No, seriously. I mean that what happened—the stuff in Charley's book—that all happened because I made a big mistake."

Stek went silent again.

"Well?" Julie prompted. "We've still got a couple of miles before we get to the magical door to fucking Never-Never Land. Tell me all about it, Stek."

Stek leaned his head back and closed his eyes. "I got involved with a group of people," he started. "After I saw some shit. I used to work at one of the FazMarts there in Golem Creek. The one that backs up to Foxend Cemetery."

Julie shivered when she heard the name. *That was where...*

"Anyway, I was at work and I wasn't even supposed to still be there. The night-shift guy was supposed to be there already. And I hear something banging around out back. So I go check it out."

They had pulled up to another red light. Blockbuster Video at 81st and Sheridan had just closed up for the night. There wasn't much traffic, even in the parking lot of the Neighborhood Market across the street. Everything seemed far more sinister than it should have. Stek seemed to be breathing more heavily.

"It was a girl, back there. Covered in blood. I was like, 'What the hell happened?' And she's freaking out, talking about a monster, a creature, something had attacked her and her friend out in the graveyard. And I'm like, 'Hey, it's all right. Come inside. Let me help you.' And she runs off, freaking out.

I go back inside." Stek heaved another deep breath as they pulled past the intersection. "I go back inside and I'm about to call the cops. Then I realize that I've got this blood all over me, and I try to wash some of it off in the bathroom. I get my jacket on to cover up what's on my shirt, and Bax Laird finally decides to show, and I just run out telling him that he's a piece of shit for being late."

They hit a patch of darkness as they passed the big hills on the west side of the street. "So I try to find her. And I tried to trace what must have been her steps, back into the graveyard. And *it's* there."

Julie felt herself shiver again. *Either he's completely nuts or he's telling me the whole truth... Charley mentions this in the book. It's why everyone at Honorius in Golem Creek thought he was crazy...*

"This...fucking...*thing*. Like a demon with big bat wings. And it's *eating* something. And I realize that it's eating this girl's *friend*." Stek winced and placed his hand over his side again. "I didn't know what to do. I kind of...I kind of went nuts. Crazy. I yelled out. And it lifts up its head, and looks right at me, and it chases me."

"It *chased* you?" Julie interjected. She hadn't realized how much she'd been drawn into the story.

"Until—long story short—it cornered me. I had no choice."

Julie waited in astonishment. "Well?" she insisted. "What did you do?"

"I punched it," Stek said flatly. "I punched it in the face. As hard as I could. And I guess it wasn't expecting that. It kind of backed off, then it gave me this hurt look on its weird, reptile face. Then it flew off."

They were approaching 101st Street, where civilization began to diminish. The darkness suddenly intensified.

"It...*flew off*?" Julie repeated. "You *hit* it? You just *punched* it? Like—*bam*!"

"Like I said," Stek opened his eyes and squinted at the road ahead, "it had me cornered."

"That's—" Julie didn't quite know what to say. "That's— fucking *cool*."

Stek grinned modestly. "Hell," he said. "If I told you that I had also pissed my pants, would it still seem as cool?"

Julie laughed. "Yes," she said. "You punched a fucking *monster*. You're allowed to piss your pants if you do that."

Stek chuckled. "Anyway, after that it was a short step to Booker and those guys, among others—hey, keep an eye out," he said. "There's a reddish-brown pole up here with an electrical box in front of it. The turnoff is just before it."

Stek fell silent. Julie decided not to pressure him to give the rest of his story—at least, not until after they'd found this portal-thing. Moments later they saw the marker and the turnoff. Julie pulled the car off the road onto a small patch of cracked asphalt with a crooked chain-link fence just beyond it.

"Looks like it's locked," Julie noted.

Stek reached into his pocket and extracted his car keys. "I think—" he flipped through the keys. "Hang on. I *think* one of these opens it. Fuckers keep cutting the goddamned thing off, even though I gave one of them the other key."

"Who?"

"Hang on. I'll be right back." Stek hopped out of the car and proceeded to unlock the fence and open it. He bowed (much like Booker would have) and waved Julie through (again, in a very similar fashion to Booker—one wonders where Booker may have gotten the notion).

Julie hesitated only briefly before shaking her head in awe at her own stupidity, then guided the Silver Fist through the gate, to the ruins of Murdock's Mansion.

From the Notebooks of
Michael Flowers

I FELL THROUGH TIME—I *saw it for what it was, at last: a ruse, a trick, sleight of invisible hands. It was the product of* fewer *dimensions, all strung together like snapshots on a veneer of continuity, the latter our own personal contribution to the show.*

Why do we assume that the world is anything more or less than precisely what we see on the illusionist's stage?

But then, what do we see?

There is something there—but we don't know what it is. The story we make up involves us, thereby granting us some kind of existence, and everyone—the world included—gets to "be."

Curwen had implied that something like this was bound to happen. That hellish tree fed on us, on the world "up here"—we were no more nor less to it than soil.

I fear that the wrong reality has been made whole.

I fear that the undying darkness secretly harbors the light, cradles it in black, deadly paws, biding its time, for purposes we could not in any way fathom.

Curwen's instruction to me was very clear: pacify the Witches— appease the Guardian of the Gate—utter the Dread Name. *The rest ought to take care of itself.*

He had left out one key element: save yourself.

Save yourself!

The bastard was tossing me into the pit! All the work, all the instruction...for what? I was to be little more than a sacrifice to Curwen's gluttony, his insatiable desire for...what?

More power? More wealth? Domination of Earth's inhabitants? Why?

I cared for none of these things. Why was I helping him...?

PART THREE

☽ ★ ☾

FROM
DUSK
'TIL
DAWN

CHAPTER 0

FRIDAY THE THIRTEENTH, PART ZERO

"NO *SCOOBY SNACKS* FOR you, you damned, dirty dog!"

The girls were cracking up as Steve rolled around on the ground in front of them, tearing at his own clothes. He caught sight of Charley stepping out of the convenience store.

"Chuck!" he shouted, leaping up. Disco Girl and Shoddy Vampirella turned to see Charley holding the liquor out before him, walking zombie-like in their direction.

"What's up with him?" Jessica asked.

Steve shook his head. "I think I know. Hang on." He jogged over to Charley on his way over and took the bag from him. "Hefty! Nice. So did you talk to Ro-Lo? What's his big plan? Does he need me to date these chicks for a while?" He waved behind him. "That's Jessica, as you know. Merely. Jessica Merely. And that super-cute vamper chick is Lolly Bergman." Steve leaned in and whispered in Charley's ear. "Apparently, her name is *Lolly-Pop* Bergman! Can you believe that shit? Hippie parents, I'm thinking."

Steve jabbed Charley, who wore a frown in the midst of his silence. "What the fuck is *up*, man? What did he say?"

Charley put his hands in his pockets and shifted his gaze to Jessica and Lolly. "Do they want to go to the Ball? 'Cause I figure, fuck it, why not? Roland's got some game-plan that he's not letting us in on."

Steve hooted and raised his fist in salute. "*Now* you're talkin', dude! See? I knew it would turn out all right. That's the best idea I've heard in weeks."

123

Back within range of Jessica and Lolly, Steve twisted off the cap of the Bacardi with a flourish. Jessica shrieked with delight, and the deeply subdued Lolly-Pop Bergman merely grinned behind her over-applied scarlet lipstick.

"I propose a *toast!*" Steve shouted.

"What are we gonna use for glasses?" Lolly asked.

"*Glasses?*" Steve said, taken aback. "Glasses, my love, are for *nerds!*" He tipped back the bottle and took several healthy gulps, to applause and laughter from the two girls.

"Gimme! Don't drink it *all!*" Jessica yelped, and grabbed the bottle from him. Steve gasped, doubled over for a moment, then cackled victoriously.

Charley, not feeling at all like joining in the fun, had already decided nonetheless to get drunk. He had begun to notice the peculiar discrepancies in his memory, just as Roland had said, gradually getting filled in as he continued to feel himself into this time and place. He glanced back at the glowing yellow Bang for Your Buck sign and the flickering fluorescent lights above the door.

I got a C in Mrs. Hurtangle's class last fall...Molly's family moved after her house burned down, didn't they...?

He couldn't see anyone sitting on the stool behind the register. Secretly, he wished for a naggin of Jameson's; he patted the back pocket of his jeans, which suddenly held the little bottle.

Thanks for nothing, Roland, he thought. Accompanied by the laughter and hysterics of the two girls and Steve Chernowski, who would probably be barfing in the gym toilets within the hour, Charley twisted off the lid of the Jameson's and followed them to Honorius.

THE CREATURE THAT BOUNDED at Stek Jarry out of the darkness of the forest, snarling and growling—and, apparently, wearing colorful jams? And a tattered T-shirt that perhaps read (at a glance, anyway) "Who Sharted?"—grazed the roof of the Honda with claws that could have shredded a stack of

Damian Stephens novels.[*]

Stek's first attempt at re-entry—leaping through the window—was fantastically unsuccessful as, alas, the window was closed. It was a lucky venture nonetheless, as his briefly stunned countenance fell just short of the creature's reach, which landed some fifteen yards distant before rolling and re-calibrating for its next attack.

"Get in, you idiot!" Julie screamed, reaching over and shoving the door open. Stek was miraculously unconcussed. He grabbed the edge of the car and was mostly in his seat before Julie floored it (an unceremonious occasion in a stick-shift vehicle designed for short jaunts in small neighbor-hoods).

"Where do I *go*, for Christ's sake?" Julie implored. Blood-curdling howls emanated from the forest around them.

Stek managed to orient himself upright again and slam shut the door. "Ah! I don't know! I mean, just follow the road—"

Julie barely swerved in time to avoid the ravenous demon—okay, the *werewolf*!—bounding across the one-way, forest-canopied lane just ahead of them...but luck, and convincing narrative, can only hold out so long. A dreaded, repetitive *thump-thump-thump* accompanied some loss of steering control—

"We've got a flat!" Julie shouted. "Fuck this!"

"Don't you have a gun or something?" Stek screamed at an astonishing pitch. Julie almost wanted to slug him.

"A gun? Who the fuck do you think I am?" Julie strained to swerve the car around a bend in the road.

"I thought you were some kind of bad ass!" Stek shouted. He had aligned himself in such a way that his arms and legs braced the dashboard and ceiling.

And then he noticed the old pile of bricks that had once been a chimney...

"There! It's right there! We can make it!"

"Where? What?" Julie held the wheel tightly and floored it.

"What are you doing?" Stek screamed.

---

[*] A difficult thing to do, since they're so *metal*, haha! (*Please stop!*)

"What do you mean?" Julie responded. A dark shape appeared, hovering against the night just beyond the old chimney. It seemed substantially larger than the monster that had attacked them moments ago—

Something shoved the car from behind.

A collective cry of astonishment, a hybrid of the expletives for fecal matter and fornication, erupted from Julie and Stek. Neither knew who spoke what, but when the car smashed into the pile of bricks, spun, upended, and fell through the earth,[*] they really did expect to slam into the ground at a rate that would preclude maintenance of physical life.

But they didn't. Not exactly.

They were upended. Stek's supertense positioning of his body had badly bruised him. Julie's use of a seatbelt had saved her from excessive damage, though her head now rested uncomfortably against the roof.

But the Honda, the Silver Fist, King of the 25 MPH Road, lay like a June bug on its carapace, wheels fruitlessly rolling against empty air.

"Stek?" Julie said as she opened her eyes. She hadn't realized that she'd been holding them shut—what instinct was it that performed said reflex? A strange notion: by shutting the eyes tightly, death might be avoided?

"Agh," a voice spoke from beside her. "Oh. Ugh."

It was Stek. He sounded roughly the same.

Julie carefully worked her way out of the tangle of her seat belt and slowly collapsed, through a sequence of hitherto unrehearsed movements, onto a patch of ground. She stood up, wobbling slightly, and breathed in the soft, somehow comforting scent of motor oil before realizing that, despite the ailing glow of headlights from her once-proud automobile, she knew not where she stood.

"Stek?"

"Still in here," came the muffled voice. "Agh. A little

---

[*] A result of cutting corners during pouring of the original foundation—specifically, ignoring the necessity of reinforcing steel and post-tensioning of the slab.

cramped, but—okay. Here I come."

Stek dragged himself out the other shattered side window.

"Are you okay?" Julie coughed out in the dusty, dark room, stepping gingerly over the remains of a shattered set of shelves that once bore lawn equipment, old flowerpots, and several gas cans.

"Ah—yes?" Stek stood up and steadied himself on the side of the car. "Where—oh, wow. Haven't seen this place in a while." He coughed into his hand.

Julie glanced around the room. It looked like a storage shed of some sort. A set of stairs led up to a sturdy-looking door on the far side. More intriguingly, a shimmering black pool hovered vertically in the midst of the room, a few feet from the back end of the Honda.

"What is—where did—oh." Julie gazed incredulously at the portal. "Oh. So that's how it works!"

Stek grinned, winced, then grinned again. "Yep. Looks like we lucked out."

"The car's totaled!" Julie observed, suddenly coming to her senses.

"Like I said: we lucked out," Stek repeated. "Amazing. The whole fucking car came through! Let's talk about transportation issues later. I suggest we get a move on. That thing works for anyone that wants to come through it—so—" He limped over to the stairs and began to climb them.

Julie hesitated. "Wait a second," she said. She returned to the driver's side door and reached in through the shattered window. *Something about this seems oddly familiar,* she thought as she extracted the keys and her backpack from the wreckage. She patted the steering wheel gently. *Goodbye, old friend...I'll try to come back for you...*

Stek gingerly cracked open the door. "It's unlocked," he whispered down to her. "That could be good or bad."

Julie's head ached where it had smacked into the roof of the car on impact, but otherwise she felt—physically, at least—in decent shape. "Where exactly are we, again?" she asked as she caught up with him, relatively certain that she knew the answer.

"A storage shed on Max Plunkett's property," Stek replied, pushing open the door and stepping through into another dark room. "Everything's coming full circle, I guess. We're back home, at least—well, if that sonofabitch doesn't shoot us on our way back to the road."

"Who would—?"

"Remember Chris Baxter?" Stek said in response.

Julie suddenly did remember "Chris Baxter"—from the *Fear Club* novel, the scene where Max Plunkett tries to shoot down everyone running for this portal, this portal in—

"Golem Creek," she said aloud. "We're here!"

"We're saying that a lot, lately." Stek chuckled, then winced again. "I may need your assistance getting across the field out there. Let's hope Old Man Plunkett's asleep."

"ONE LEATHERFACE, ONE JASON Voorhees—make that two Jason Voorheeses—is that how you'd plural it? Freddy Krueger. Stupid sweater—too clean! *Too clean, dude*! Awesome gloves, though. Aw, hell—check it out, dude! Sexy witch! Two—*three*—holy Christ, *four* sexy witches—"

Steve's running census of Monster Ball attendees had begun the moment he and Charley realized that neither of them had tickets, nor money for tickets. Jessica and Lolly-Pop had insisted they would be able to get the two of them in—and promptly disappeared into the crowd. *With* the booze.

The two dreamworld veterans, newly returned to their home front, had tried calling Julie at home from a payphone outside Bang for Your Buck. Steve had left a message indicating (with a wink at Charley, who saw nothing particularly ingenious about it) that they would "meet Julie at the Monster Ball as we planned." They now sat on a small hill across from the decorated entrance gate of their old high school, feeling the relentless *thump-thump-thump*[*] of The Borgo Pass as they rocked out inside and engaged in hoping that Plan B—"Julie shows up"—would come to fruition.

"What if she's chained up or something?" Charley asked.

---

[*] Did this just happen...?

"Well, then, I guess we're in luck," Steve said. "That would mean she's alive. So if we don't run into her at the Ball, we rescue her at her house! Then raid the fridge."

Charley finally found the opening he needed to ask a question he'd had on his mind for years. "So, you and Julie? Are like...I mean, it's like you're best friends—but you..." He realized he didn't *quite* know how to put into words what had seemed so apparent to him moments before.

Steve shook his head. "You don't get it, man," he said, pulling up clumps of grass at random. "There are things in nature that *have* to be a certain way, even if they don't want to."

Charley shook his head. "Not following," he said. "Give me one example."

"Easy," Steve said. "Julie and me we're like—we're like sodium and chlorine. You ever see what happens when you put sodium and chlorine together? *Bang*! And that's, like, salt. Right there. Sodium might want to hang out in a library all day and read; chlorine might want to fill up a locker-room full of jocks and gas them to death." He chuckled. "But in the end, despite the explosions, they've gotta find each other, because they know that otherwise you can't get that essential stuff you need for margaritas and shit."

Charley laughed.

Steve was clearly too amused by the crowds of partygoers to elaborate much further. "Anyway, what's the rush, man? She's probably inside, or on her way. We'll catch up with her!"

Charley sighed again in resignation. "Fuck it, man. You're right. Or you're wrong, maybe. But what else are we gonna do?"

Charley had expected some sort of adrenaline-overdrive effect from finding himself suddenly beset with tons of people after what seemed like months living in near-isolation, but it turned out to feel very much akin to recovering from a cold: it just kind of "happened." All of a sudden, there you were: in the world, nothing special, as if nothing had happened... Indeed, he kept having the sense that he was missing something, some key piece of the puzzle, like having a dream and remembering most of it...but there was some part, some *really important part* that just kept slipping away...

"Steve? Do you remember something else? About Roland? And maybe...a *carpet*, maybe? I don't know."

Steve didn't seem to hear the question. He chuckled as one of the sexy witches—noticeably stumbling as a result of pre-show indulgence—deigned to blow Steve a kiss, to the obvious chagrin of her boyfriend, whose costume didn't flatter him. Was the guy trying to be Superman? Or Clark Kent wearing a cape?

"Dude, check out those guys over there," Steve said, nudging Charley's shoulder. "Look at the cloud coming out of that blunt! Damn it!"

"Is that just us in the future?" Charley said, and leaned his head back against the cool grass. *Just relax, keep thinking about it, it'll come back to you...*

Steve shook his head. "I sure hope so," he said. *The uncowed, unbendable Steve Chernowski, ladies and gentlemen, once and future king of a world that never existed...*

"Are there any non-sexy versions of costumes?" Charley asked as a sexy Princess Leia walked past.

Steve looked at him, aghast. "Curb thy tongue, blasphemer!" he said. "It's all right," he continued to the half-clad Leia, who ignored him. "He's fucking stupid."

Charley patted his pockets. *Didn't bring any magic keys or magic books or...oh, well, here's a pack of Zig-Zags...* "So, Lolly-Pop and Jessica aren't coming back?" he observed.

Steve snorted. "Don't know what they're *missing*, man! To hell with 'em."

"But *we're* the ones left out here," Charley reminded him. "Roland was pretty clear about something being up." He sighed. "And this Weston Gray guy? Or monster? Or whatever?"

"*Leave Weston Gray to me,*" Steve said rigidly, then broke into laughter. "Just kidding. First of all, so what? So he's a monster. Not like we haven't seen *that* before. Why be racist about it?"

"Yeah, but—"

"But *what*, man? We just spent the past Christ-knows-how-many months kind-of trapped in the equivalent of a super-cool, infinitely awesome prison with no bars. And I'm starting to feel pretty confident that we can just head right back once this place starts to get irritating again, as I have no doubt it will. I have learned *many things* during my tenure as a small god."

Charley laughed. "Such as?"

"You don't need to have special powers just to chill out, for one," he responded. "And if you're getting bored, it's because you haven't gone far enough!"

Steve's grinning countenance was suddenly replaced with a look of disgust as he turned his attention back to the Monster Ball entrance. "Aw, come *on!* Are you *serious?* Are you supposed to be a *werewolf* or fucking *Chewbacca*, man?"

Wolfman Chewie barely had time to respond to the insult before Steve moved on to the attendee behind him.

"Oh! Look! Look! Dude!" Steve started clapping and hooting. "Hell, yeah! *SURRENDER, DOROTHY! Tonight's the night!*" He broke down laughing as a girl in a sexy Dorothy Gale outfit gave him the finger on her way into the Ball.

"These chicks, you know?" Steve said, chuckling.

Charley shook his head. "Which of these people are *monsters...?*" he asked the sky. The stars twinkled in response; the spring sky was clear, lucid. The moon, superbly full, had just crested one of the circular turrets on Honorius High's roof. That's when Charley saw the humanoid shape crouching there like some sort of gargoyle.

"Woah! Check out that—"

"I know, I *know*, honey, butchuh *cain't* always *GIT* whutchuh *WOHNT!*" Steve sang.

Charley found shortly that he was pointing at nothing but the moon. Steve turned to him, a look of sympathy on his face.

"They're down *there*, Chuck," he said, gently angling Charley's hand toward the entrance. "It's okay. We're all behind you on this." He burst into laughter.

Charley shrugged and lay back down on the grass, dimly aware that The Borgo Pass had just started in on their set of alternating Black Sabbath hits and fan favorites.

"AH, BUT THIS IS only *half* of me!" Molly's voice rang out from her throne, risen on the shoulders of six distressingly athletic and mostly naked young men.

" 'Half,' my Queen?" spoke Farmer McNabb hesitantly from his perch on the litter beside her. "Hardly 'half,' your Majesty! Never and in no way ever 'half'—"

"You *know* what I mean!" Molly's voice brooked no argument. Dozens of petals from various species of extinct flora rained from her crown as she swatted a bee. "*Where* is that unrepentant, silly, ugly, hateful bastard!"

Farmer McNabb, unwilling—perhaps unable, at this point in his masterfully obsequious career—to *not* answer, began to perform the vocal activity known as "hemming and hawing," a universe-spanning behavior amongst the weak-willed.

Molly's frown grew a frown. She thrust a hand to her left and made a slight clicking sound with her luxuriously manicured fingernails. Seconds later a flute of ambrosial champagne appeared. She quaffed it in a single, elegant gulp before tossing the glass at a passing tree.

"The college is utterly *yours*, of course, Your Majesty..." Farmer McNabb began, his anxiety rising at the inadequacy of his response even as his voice fell. Molly didn't even deign to glance at him.

Yes, Golem Creek University had been taken utterly— the fools from Roland's habitat across the way[*] had cracked the lock in that blasted dungeon at last,[†] but something *else* had happened, too...or perhaps *not enough* had happened. She was, indeed, the "Molly Furnival" that knew—at least for the moment—that she *was*, in fact, Molly Furnival, Queen of Færy. The deal she'd struck for more "stuffing," for something more permanent than *this*, was *supposed* to have worked by *now*...it was all so—

---

[*] Please forgive the deeply incapable metaphors.
[†] *Vide* Steve, Charley, and Julie's literally unwritten recovery of the key behind the "trapdoor" in Book One.

"Goddamned *irritating*!" Molly shouted. Farmer McNabb cringed. Her *douloi* hesitated only minutely in their labors.

But the chaos of orgiastic activity over and through which she surfed in queenly decorum merely intensified, being, after all, a manifestation of her emotional fervor in "people" form. The lawns and parks and sidewalks and stoops of all the buildings on the grounds of Golem Creek University thronged and burst and creaked with the weight of wildness Molly's enchantments had unleashed here...

"Get me to that *Ball*!" Molly shouted. "And get me something *stronger than that grape-piss to drink*!"

IT WAS THE EASTER Bunny, paused for some reason on the shoulder of Edgewood Road, that finally handed sanity's regretful RSVP to Julie.

"Stek, that's fucking *nuts*," Julie whispered from their cover in the weeds beside the road. "Please do *not* brain that creature!"

Besides two drunken pot-shots angled roughly in their direction and a single, incomprehensible redneck shout of Confederate glee before passing out (presumably from inhaling a case of PBR), Stek and Julie had not been mauled or molested by Max Plunkett on their way off his property. The streets of Golem Creek on the other side of Chicken Hill, whose long bulk rose and continued off to their right, were dark, however. Parents cowered in the gloom of their homes as their children harnessed hell in the handbasket of Honorius High.

Stek had, in the semi-darkness, tripped over a length of what appeared to be lead pipe in the tall grass at the edges of Max Plunkett's property. Such things were never out of place in the unkempt lawns of alcoholic pagans such as Max Plunkett; indeed, Julie was surprised he hadn't come across a loaded gun. A weapon, at any rate, seemed like a sensible thing to have in their presently perilous time.

"We need a ride!" Stek said irritably. "What do you want me to do?"

"It's a fucking *costume*, dude! What is your problem?" Julie responded. "You skulk around in shadows and take the most *difficult* possible route to getting things done. I mean, no fucking wonder you're in so much trouble all the time. Just *ask*—"

"Sh! He's heading this direction!"

"Don't you *dare*—"

"*Sh!*"

The moon was full, but the light it shed over their trek to the road made everything appear dubious and phantasmic. The Easter Bunny seemed to be looking for something, muttering to itself and occasionally chomping on a carrot clutched in one oversized paw.

Julie could have sworn she heard Stek giving himself a pep talk under his breath. *This is ridiculous*, she thought, and stood up, earning several half-quelled shouts of protest from Stek.

"Excuse me!" Julie shouted. The Bunny turned its head and comical body in her direction. *Boy, that looks awfully realistic...* "Hey! Easter Bunny? Yeah. Um. My buddy and I. We need a ride."

Stek had flattened himself utterly to the ground.

"*Get up!*" Julie whispered harshly at him. Stek began gradually creeping away in response.

The Easter Bunny was now perhaps twenty yards away from them. The ice cream truck it had exited lay some ten yards behind it, parked and idling on the shoulder of the road.

Julie smiled as convincingly as possible. "I'm sorry. My name's Julie—"

That a bipedal bunny rabbit could make such a screeching, ear-shattering wail Julie would never previously have thought nor guessed. It launched itself toward her, its oversized rabbit feet capably bounding in her direction. Julie froze in an attempt to scream—

—and a shot rang out in the night, temporarily deafening her. For a moment, she didn't notice the hail of what appeared to be shimmering, neon-colored jelly beans raining down on her in the moonlight. For that same moment, she barely noticed the thud of the Easter Bunny's six-foot-tall body as it slammed into the earth in front of her, sending up a spray of dust and pebbles.

As time reasserted itself in her vicinity, she gazed down at the body. It quivered once before the carrot held by its massive paw dropped to the ground and rolled into the grass.

"Don't worry," Stek said from behind her. "I mean, if you're worried that I just killed the Easter Bunny. There's a bunch of them. Booker told me that they once had to flame-throw a busload of them."

"Why did you—where—"

Stek came up beside her, grinning. "Shotgun, whaddaya know?" he said. "*Wow*! Both loaded *and* didn't blow me up!"

"You *said* it was a—"

"Lead pipe, of course," Stek finished. "Why make you nervous unnecessarily? Anyway, let's get to the van—"

Before he could finish his statement, the van sped off.

"God*damn*it!" Stek shouted, chasing briefly after its fading taillights. He stopped, cursed again, grimaced at the sudden sharp pain in his side, and headed back to Julie, who now knelt, still basically frozen, before the giant bunny's corpse.

"Hey, I'd help you bury it, but we don't really have time for that—"

"Just—" Julie seemed like a dam about to burst. Stek silenced himself. Julie grabbed a handful of the bunny's jelly-bean innards and held them up in the moonlight. "Please don't fire a gun that close to me again."

"I just *saved*—" Stek paused and took a breath. "Right. Of course. Right-o!" He turned back to the road.

"Mourn all you want," he said, contemplating their next move. "But don't eat any of those jelly beans. They'll fuck you up. Totally hallucinogenic."

"Eh! Yo! Wake up, Charley!"

Steve was shaking him awake. *When had he fallen asleep...?*

"Check out the Doc Brown, dude! He even drove up in a fucking *DeLorean*!"

And indeed he had. Charley was unsure of whether or not he had simply begun dreaming a new version of the world, once again—*dreams within dreams within dreams...* Sure enough, someone who was *nearly* the spitting image of Dr. Emmett Brown had just exited a DeLorean at the far end of the parking lot and proceeded to stride purposefully toward the two figures on the hill (one of whom had apparently passed out).

"That's fucking classic," Steve announced happily. "I wonder who that is? Is that Mr. Fandolini? Wearing a wig, maybe? Sweet."

The Monster Ball had officially reached epic proportions. The majority of the teenaged population of Golem Creek—perhaps even *all* the teenaged population of Golem Creek—was now grinding away in ghoulish ecstasy to The Borgo Pass as they banged out "Symptom of the Universe."

Steve stood up. "I'm officially fucking bored," he said. "I can't believe it."

"No Julie?" Charley asked, rubbing his eyes.

"No *Julie*, man!" Steve said. "We should have seen her by now. Maybe she's out back?" He frowned. "I wonder if she's maybe not even, you know, *here*? In Golem Creek? I mean, her answering machine message was the same old robot voice, but—I don't know."

Charley felt a familiar sense of anxiety coupled with guilt twist his insides. "Shit," he said. "*Shit*. Steve, what if she's—"

"Woah, check it out!" Steve said, pointing back at Doc Brown and the two druggies. "Looks like *someone's* getting detention!"

Doc Brown appeared to be waving his arms emphatically as he announced something to the conscious member of the duo. The other guy appeared to still be passed out.

"That's what we need," Charley suddenly announced.

"What?" Steve pulled a crushed pack of Camel Wides out of his pocket and opened it. "Oh, come on. Now of all times? Should've gone with nonfilters. Everyone knows those packs are endless."

"A *time machine*," he said, standing up and waving toward the DeLorean. "We need a *time machine*."

"Maybe Roland's got one," Steve suggested, sparking and failing to light his Bic several times. "Fuck. *Et tu*, lighter?" He glanced around. "I'm gonna run over to the Courtyard and see if I can bum a smoke. Might be able to get in through the back if it's anyone we know. Hang tight, Joe Schmoe."

Steve jogged off toward the other end of the school. Charley looked back at the incipient conflagration between Doc Brown and the two druggies. There the DeLorean sat; all three characters had gone, presumably into the school by way of the side entrance near Principal Patterson's office.

There the DeLorean sat...

"I wish—man, I *wish* I had a time machine just like that DeLorean," Charley said to the air, the night, and the strains of "Love Song" by The Damned suddenly sounding from deep within the halls of Honorius High.

"STEVE?"

It was Petzi Perez. She was partially obscured by darkness, but the scent of tobacco was strong on her—here he would find his light, by this Angel of Darkness. Seriously: she was clad in a great black shroud beset with dark wings, her face painted a ghastly white, her eyes ringed about with kohl (or at least black face paint).

"Peez! By the gods, I'm glad I found you!" Steve sprinted up the steps toward her.

"You want to bum a smoke, right?"

"A genius *and* an angel!" Steve asserted.

"You'll have to make do with Salem Menthols," Peez said.

Steve's smile faltered briefly, then reasserted itself. " 'Make do,' love? Hardly!"

Peez snorted and handed him a lung-crystallizing menthol cigarette and a Zippo.

"So," she said. "What're you supposed to be?"

Steve took several puffs off the cigarette and grinned. "William Shakespeare," he said. "Reincarnated. Have you seen Julie?"

"Who?" Peez responded as Steve handed back her Zippo. Steve's heart clenched at the implications of the response—*she didn't hear you, just push right on past it*—

"How's the Monster Ball this year?" he asked as nonchalantly as he could.

"Pretty sweet," Peez said. "I scored some kind bud off Tom Fallow. And a bunch of that stuff."

Steve stood for a moment, perplexed. "Tom Fallow? What about Pete? And what stuff?"

"Pete's in there," she answered. "But I think he smoked all his profits. He was blissed out, listening to something on a *Walkman*, right next to the stage."

Steve chuckled. "Good 'ol Streetwise Pete," he said. "What's this 'stuff,' again?"

"Oooh," Peez responded, taking Steve's hand sensuously. "You *gotta* try that. *Everybody's* been on it. Tom's been giving out free samples!"

"Tom Fallow," Steve said thoughtfully. "I don't think I've met him."

"You should," Peez said. She was clearly stoned, and leaned up against Steve. "He's basically been The Man for the past three months. 'Candyman' some people call him. 'Cause of the hearts. Not like Pete's even *trying* to compete. Pete. Compete. Ha."

"Sounds like *someone's* been sampling the merchandise!" Steve laughed. "Got any, I don't know, you feel like—"

"Gone," she said, and stepped suddenly away toward the door. "All gone. I think. Ha. Like Sturges and his buddies. Ha. Ha." Her weird dark laugh made Steve think twice about indulging. He decided, on second thought, that he would probably go ahead and at least try to score some weed, if he could find this Tom Fallow character and convince him of the rightness of supporting inveterate cannabis users.

Peez stubbed out her cigarette and stepped back through the door, which had been propped open with her plastic scythe. "You coming?" she asked.

Steve grinned. "Well, of *course*," he said, and followed her in.

JIM BUSKEY AND BAX Laird sat in the cramped custodial chambers at Honorius High, trying desperately to empty a half-gallon of peppermint schnapps.

"Ugh," Bax said. "This stuff tastes like fucking mouthwash."

"All I could find at short notice," Jim said, finding some difficulty in executing the complicated transitions between palato-alveolar and alveolar articulations.*

"Yeah, well, you should raid Walt's liquor stash once he passes out," Bax suggested.

"It's not more *liquor* we need," Jim said, lifting a nearly empty plastic cup of schnapps before him.

Bax nodded his head. "I know, I know," he said. They were waiting—had been waiting, ever since dispatching "Dandy" Andy—for some sign that PyGoLiRo had acknowledged the favor. Meanwhile, the final part of their agreement had been confirmed with the appearance of *Khephra* at the last murder— or feasting—site. "Tom's here somewhere. He wouldn't miss this. Last chance dance, and all."

Jim chuckled. "Damned if I don't feel sorry for the guy," Jim admitted, refilling his cup before it was empty.

"No shit," Bax said. "If it wasn't for the ticket out of here, I'd probably just make friends with him. Get good discount weed and all, you know?"

They heard The Borgo Pass's dramatic conclusion of "Love Song." Then they heard an equally ungodly sound, like something clambering down the hallway. It emitted a blood-curdling growl just outside the door of the custodian's office.

"Showtime," Jim said, smiling. "They're meeting on the roof. To absorb more moonlight, I guess." He drained his cup.

Bax grinned as convincingly as he could in return—but he hadn't had *nearly* enough alcohol to match Jim's confidence level. How many times does a horde of uncaged, feral carnivores ignore a random guy like him? Even if he did have "official" immunity?

He grimaced and downed the last of his schnapps.

STEK'S THREE ATTEMPTS TO flag down a car all met with failure before Julie decided they ought to check her house.

---

* The "sh" and "n" and "t" sounds. (You let me through for *that*?!)

"*Your* house?" Stek seemed flabbergasted. "But isn't it two blocks *that* way? We need to go *this* way!"

"What do you think the chances are that reality has *another* copy of my car here?" she asked. "I mean, come on. I've been *two versions* of myself before!"

Stek stopped walking along the shoulder of South Street, incredulous. He tapped the shotgun idly on his boot. The chamber had held exactly one shot, which he supposed could be considered miraculous or unlucky, depending on how you looked at it.

At any rate, he could still use it as a bludgeoning instrument, if the need arose.

"You *were*?" he asked. "How the hell did that happen?"

"Long story. Doesn't matter. The point is that my—her—our car is probably just *sitting* there." Julie reached into her pocket. "And I've got the keys."

Stek thought for a moment. "Huh," he said. "No chance you're out for the night, for some reason?"

"Stek, I don't *go* out," she answered. "Besides, aren't you noticing it yet?"

Stek knew exactly what she was hinting at: the sensation of his brain adapting and re-writing its history in light of their "new" presence. Somehow, he *knew* (despite an undeniable certainty that his brown Camaro was parked *somewhere* within range of Honorius) there *was* no other Stek here...at least, not any more...

"There's no other you here," he said.

"There was a distinct sensation of having another 'me,' the last time," she said. "And it's true: I'm not getting that sense now."

"But that could also mean—"

"True. It could mean there's no me *at all* here. Which means—"

"We're basically strangers in a strange land," he finished. "Or strangers in a familiar land. Or whatever."

Julie nodded. "Let's cut through Ballard Park," she suggested, pointing to the streetlamp by the park entrance just up ahead.

When they reached the entrance, Julie hopped the low wooden perimeter fence.

"Huh," Stek said again, before following her a beat later.

"What now?"

"That sign said 'MacArthur's.' Pretty clearly. Not 'Ballard.' Just so you know."

Julie emphatically shrugged in an attempt to divest herself of the nervousness following immediately from Stek's observation.

"Everything *looks* the same," she commented.

Stek nodded uncertainly.

They were halfway across the lawn that backed up to her neighborhood when the night sky erupted with light.

Stek fell backwards in astonishment. "What the—"

"It's—" Julie watched as the miracle in the firmament disappeared almost as quickly as it had appeared.

"It was a *rainbow*," Stek whispered, daring to speak. "Julie, that was a *fucking*—"

"Rainbow?" Julie said. "Did you see where it came from?"

Stek lifted himself from the ground and brushed off his jeans. "There," he said, pointing.

"That's Brake Street," Julie said. She turned, pointing at the path it had taken. "And it ended up right there. Must have ended somewhere near the top of Chicken Hill."

They looked at each other, then turned to face the slope of Chicken Hill, abode of the Murk.

"Wait a second," Julie uttered quietly. "Do you see that?"

Stek was nodding his head as he backed up unconsciously. "I see it," he said. "That's a *lot* of something dark and scary, Julie. We should probably—uh—"

"*Run!*" she shouted.

They made it through the dense thicket of woods behind Julie's neighborhood, losing only the shotgun in the process (to Stek's curses). They made it through the alleyway that separated the woods from the front of the outlying properties. They made it on to Julie's street.

And a flash, like a ball of lightning, hurtled toward them as they approached her house.

STEVE WAS AMAZED AND nearly overwhelmed by the grinding masses of drug-addled teenagers that flocked, huddled, danced, cavorted, and generally screamed at each other for no apparent reason except unbridled release of energy. He *thought* he saw a teacher or two around...although, like most years, they were probably as wasted as everyone else.

He lost Peez somewhere between the nearly empty English hall beside the Courtyard and his attempt to get *back* to the *goddamned front* of the *goddamned building*. He also stopped saying "excuse me" and "pardon," opting to shove and scramble relentlessly.

He did not come across Pete Jarry—although a promising candidate was someone in a full Godzilla suit with a gigantic cigar sticking out of its mouth, lounging drunkenly on its side by a Coke machine. He *did* see several acquaintances, including Prasad Veerma dressed as what could only be an Indian David Lee Roth, sharing a flask with someone whose iconic red-and-white guitar, slung over his back, must have identified him as Eddie van Halen.

But no Julie.

It was Charley, of all people—dressed in a pretty sharp-looking *Blues Brothers* getup and wearing a kid's Frankenstein mask—who finally stopped Steve. He removed his mask, grinning uncontrollably.

"Chuck! What the *hell*, man? Where'd you pilfer the duds?" Steve shouted above the crowd in an attempted, and terrible, cockney accent. The Borgo Pass was midway through "Evil" by Mercyful Fate, and the noise level was unbearable—he figured he could get away with it.

Charley grabbed Steve's Iron Maiden T-shirt and dragged him behind a stairwell occupied only by what *appeared* to be two Fairy Girls[*] coupling furiously. Despite the Room of Their Own, it would have to do.

Steve stared unblinkingly at the proceedings of elvish lust

---

[*] Note the differentiated spelling. The Old English "æ" ("ash") has here been modernized. (Stop this!!!)

as Charley spoke.

"You're not going to *believe* this shit!" Charley shouted.

"Oh, I'm gonna believe it," Steve said. "Trust me. Spill it."

"No, seriously," Charley said. "You're not. Because I just got back, and it was basically amazing. No, man, it wasn't just 'amazing,' it was—"

"Did you run into Julie?" Steve asked.

"Yes! Yes I did. She's outside with Stek, waiting."

Steve tore his eyes from the ravenous lesbians and stared at Charley. "With *Stek Jarry*?!"

Charley nodded vigorously. "They're out by the DeLorean—"

"Okay, okay, clearly I missed something," Steve said. "DeLorean. Mr. Fandolini's car? Let's get out in the open and—wait. With *Stek*? That fucking guy is *dead*, dude!"

"I know! I mean, he *was*! I mean—hold on. Look, we've *really* got to get out of here right now. But *check this out*."

Charley reached into his blazer and pulled out a tattered old paperback book, its cover lettering barely discernible in the dim orange glow from the hall.

Steve moved in closer to get a better look at it. "*Fear Club*?" he read aloud. The cover depicted three people around a grave on a hill, a monstrous form writhing in the midst of them. "That's—wait a second. That's—"

"*Us*," Charley finished for him. "Me, you, and Julie."

"Then *that's*—"

"Michael Flowers," Charley said, grinning. "But get this. I think I know what to do now—"

"Hang on," Steve said, unconsciously patting his pockets for a cigarette. "Hang on. This book is the one *you* wrote."

Charley nodded, still grinning, and pointed to his name on the cover.

"You called it *Fear Club*?" Steve said. "That's a *terrible* title!"

Charley's grin faltered. "It's not *that* bad—"

Steve started laughing. "No, dude, trust me—it *sucks*!" The Borgo Pass had finished their Mercyful Fate tribute. Someone in the audience started screaming for them to play a Misfits medley. "Why didn't you call it *All Hell Breaks Loose*? Or *Gate-*

ways to Annihilation? Or—"

Charley shoved the book back in his jacket. "I guess because I'm so good at writing *full books* in order to try to send a message to *our best friend* who could be in *mortal danger* that I forgot all about how to come up with titles, dude. Fuck you."

Steve leaned in and gave him a rapid, forceful hug, which Charley gradually gave in to. "Sorry, dude. I'm sorry. I just *do* this. It's my job," Steve said.

"Well, at least I got *that* part right," Charley responded.

"Let's go hook up with the ol' ball-and-chain!" Steve shouted. He turned briefly to the undaunted Fairy Girls still locked in erotic oblivion. "We'll catch you girls later. Stay super-duper!"

Steve started working his way through the crowd of goblins and monsters and sexy nurses/witches/vampiresses/ werecats/succubi-in-general, checking periodically to make sure that Charley was following him before he was, inevitably, turned around in the process.

The Misfits kicked in—"I Turned Into a Martian." Brandon Fertig, lead singer of The Borgo Pass, did a passable Danzig imitation. The crazed lighting in the room began flickering as the effects people started a pretty neat trick that made it look like dark, wraith-like shadows were flooding in through the vents above.

Steve had shoved his way past a small knot of frantic dancers before he realized he had lost track of Charley. He turned to a sexy...well, she appeared to be a sexy *prostitute*, for all intents and purposes, and smiled at her.

She opened her mouth—most likely to shriek some unearned insult at him, he suspected—and one of the wraiths *flew in.*

The process took perhaps two seconds, long enough for a gasp of astonishment, after which she smiled back at him, *with a mouthful of dripping fangs—*

Steve screamed. He would reflect later that this reaction, girlish and unthinking at the time, was a perfectly acceptable response to the situation. The tart attempted to grab him. His instincts dropped him like a rag-doll.

Sensei would be proud, Steve thought, and began crawling on all fours, as fast as he could, in the direction he *thought* would lead to an exit from the main hall. The growls and roars and increased viciousness of the dancers around him seemed to indicate that something had gone terribly wrong.

Someone—correction, some*thing*—grabbed him from the middle. He felt himself quite suddenly lifted into the air, and the scene unfolded about him: black wraiths entering partygoers with full abandon, a swirling chaos of possession.

Whatever had captured him somehow lost its hold. He fell, kicking, punching, and shouting, into a hungry swarm of once-sexy nurses with no apparent intention of saving his life.

CHARLEY LOST TRACK OF Steve within seconds.

"Steve!" he shouted, to no avail. *I told him we're headed out front...he won't miss the DeLorean...*

Charley pushed, prodded, slid by, and generally forced his way through the mass. The music increased in intensity as dancers started shuddering like one-too-many moles of gas in a compression chamber. In a burst of effort, he exited the room through a set of closed doors—into the *wrong hall*, the small one leading back to the math classrooms.

Shit.

It was populated, but mostly by couples looking for a break from the madness in the gym. The music still pounded away, nearly as loud, the treble thankfully diminished in intensity.

Charley paused for a moment to orient himself, then proceeded at a fast walk. *All the way back, past the big bathrooms at the end of the hall, then cut around and take the exit by the band room—if it's even unlocked—*

Shattered planks of wood smacked him down against the glistening marble floor before he heard the roar and crunch of fists that caused it. He slid several feet, stood up instinctively, ignoring the fiery pain in his lower back, and glanced down as blood splattered across the floor from somewhere behind him.

Screams followed this, presumably from the hapless couples in the hall, and Charley sprinted forward, not bothering to try to catch a glimpse of what was behind him, simply *running*—

He stumbled and slipped at the end of the hall, banging into the men's bathroom door resoundingly.

The hall leading to the band-room exit was occupied by a writhing, tentacled darkness filling it utterly. A shrill whining sound coupled with the wet smacking of its unearthly appendages flopping mindlessly against floor and walls and ceiling.

The way forward was blocked. The way back was—

Another growling rumble accompanied further screams. Charley chanced a look back at the blood-spattered hall, only to witness the heroically muscled abnormality that had smashed its way in—a singular beast, strangely sporting a red-and-white patterned guitar strapped to its flexing back, and looking for all the world like Eddie van Halen in a demonic Hulk suit—end the shrieking life in its hands: once a young man in a clown outfit, his makeup smeared by the kisses of some harlequin paramour, now little more than shreds of dripping meat, his multicolored wig a travesty of the joyful token it once was.

The only option was the toilet.

Charley wrenched open the bathroom door and flung himself in. There was a flimsy lock on the other side of the door, but no windows, although this hall backed up to the track field on the other side of the school.

There was, however, a person present, standing at the first sink and staring blankly at himself—*itself*—in the mirror.

Weston Gray blinked slowly, twice, as Charley burst into the room and saw *it* in all its glory reflected back at him. The thing, the reptilian, spike-horned nether-creature, gazed at itself with lizard eyes. On Charley's side of the mirror, it was Weston Gray, a geeky James Dean; on the other side—

The door behind Charley cracked with enough force to break his trance. He ran the only direction he could—past Weston, to the end of the room, to the last stall—

Maybe it'll eat him *instead?!?* Charley thought frantically. He slid into the stall, slamming the door shut and standing on the toilet, crouched and ready for a final confrontation.

One further hammering was all it took to shatter the bathroom door and allow his pursuer to gain entrance. A bestial roar of triumph preceded the appearance of its wicked claws over the door to Charley's stall, which ripped away from its hinges like so much aluminum foil, taking several of the remaining stall partitions to the side with it.

Batshit crazy, the slavering beast raised massive fists like knots of gnarled and twisted oak.

Its voice came like grinding stones. *"Where is Damian Stephens?"*

Charley cowered in the corner of the bathroom, feeling the twin pulsations of his heartbeat and the drums from the rave down the hall.

"I don't know who you're talking about!" Was that true, though? Did the demonic metalhead know something he didn't?

The thing—but let's call him by his assumed name, "Edward van Halen"—let out a shriek sounding like thousands of groupies flung at once from a tenth-story hotel window.

Where the battle axe came from Charley had no idea. It was, quite suddenly, simply *there* in his hand, seeming real enough, but weighing no more than would its plastic, toy-store equivalent. Charley looked frantically toward the exit. Weston— now looking decidedly more like a Weston/Satan hybrid in an untarnished black tuxedo with a freshly bloomed blood-red rose in the lapel—gazed at him with a look of bored amusement in its piercing, icy-blue eyes.

It was the look an Olympian god would give to his chance entertainment for the day. *Well?* it seemed to say. *Are you going to regale me, or not?*

Charley shut his eyes tightly and swung the axe at Eddie van Halen with everything he had.

He missed.

THE BALLAD OF CANNIBAL CORPSE

JIM THE JANITOR STOOD awkwardly on the roof, feigning calm. Bax didn't even try.

"I feel a little, uh, *out of my element*, man!" Bax whispered to Jim. The lycanthropes had gathered on the school roof for some sort of pre-carnival ritual or team meeting—Jim couldn't quite remember through the fog of drink what it was that Yassiz had said.

Bax stared anxiously at the sinister flocking of wolfmen (and -women, too?) in the moonlight. Their howls ceased abruptly. Low growls and the deep, sawblade panting of bloodthirsty animals remained. Shutting his eyes only made it worse, and seemed to intensify the musty odor of the hybrid creatures.

Jim pressed a half-empty flask into Bax's chest wordlessly. Bax took it in hope that the fire in his throat would distract him from the water in his bowels.

An ear-piercing howl suddenly erupted from the center of the congregation, followed by a travesty of human speech punctuated by growls and harsh-breathing pauses.

"Brothers and sisters of the Hollow... The sacrifices must be made... The Black God returns... His promise is kept..."

The snarling monster lifted from somewhere among his fellows the unconscious form of a young girl in (predictably enough) a sexy Catholic-schoolgirl uniform. Bax barely held back a gasp.

"What are they *doing*?" he whispered to Jim.

149

Jim shushed him with a wave of his hand...but was that a *low chuckle* Bax heard emitted from his friend's unconscionable grin?

The creatures salivated and groaned, some whimpered, some barked softly. Their leader snapped and growled at a few who dared reach for some choice cut of the delectable entrée.

Their fever seemed to reach a barely contained peak, at which point the alpha tore into the girl, then howled in triumph, flinging the body into the pack's midst. Bax could *swear* he had seen a brief attempt by the girl to fend one of them off before being occluded by the ravenous lot.

A brume of blood wafted above the crowd before a cloud, dark and menacing, became discernible overhead, a cyclone of shadows blotting out the night sky, crowning the murderous Mass before suddenly funneling downward, disappearing through the pack and into the roof.

Unearthly howls flowed like lava through Bax's body, vibrating the night air with violence. The pack dispersed, hurtling themselves across the roof and over the building's edges. Bax caught a glimpse of Jim grinning madly at the supernatural display.

What the fuck did I get myself into? Bax thought. "Now we wait?" he said, trying to mask the crippling fear in his voice.

"Now we wait," Jim said. "They'll bring us some proof that the witch has been subdued. Then we can deliver her to the rich kids back in T-Town."

"And then?" Bax asked. Screams and shrieks began issuing from below, bursting forth here and there like leaks in a dam.

"No more janitorial work," Jim said, his smile broadening. "No more *work*, period!"

CHAOS CAN BE RELIED upon to turn on itself as often as it disrupts the best-laid plans of dudes like Steve Chernowski. Not that he had a plan; he certainly had the thought: *Never know what to expect! Tell Steve one year ago that he'd be fighting to get* out *of a cluster of sexy nurses all thirsting for his blood and he'd've clocked you...*

There *were* some bites, some scratches, some extraordinary

glimpses of thoroughly unobscured undergarments—but in the end, Steve found himself thrust beneath someone *else's* bloodied corpse. He would have breathed a deeper sigh of relief, were it not for the intensity of Scotch fumes emanating from the corpulent mass lodged between him and Dracula's Nurses.

"Principal Patterson...?" Steve did his best to check for a pulse before the corpse took a deep breath.

"*Insolence! Dress code! Ah! Ah! Flags! Fifth period!*" Walter J. Patterson shrieked as the crowd of nurses descended upon him. "*By God! The PAIN! America! I've given you ALL and now I'm—AHHHH—*"

Steve ducked under a partially collapsed cafeteria table, cringing at Principal Patterson's attempt to determine his own last words. He scrambled forward in darkness and made it yards closer to the exit door before being winded by another falling body, screaming for mercy.

"*Wendy! PLEASE! I'm BEGGING you!*"

Steve twisted himself around and inadvertently kicked the bloodied Fairy Girl right into the insatiable grip of her snarling Dark Fairy Lover. Simultaneously, The Borgo Pass—looking much more like bipedal rodents now and, strangely, having improved their showmanship and dancing skills—decided to launch back into some Sabbath, with "Supernaut" as a follow-up to "Horror Business."

"I'm *sorry*! I'm sorry!" he apologized to the wailing fairy, leaping and hurtling himself toward one of the exit doors, which conveniently opened.

He flew through it, right into the arms of—

"*Julie?!?*"

They landed in a heap. Steve pushed himself up from the floor to gaze into Julie's magnificent blue eyes.

Stek shoved a broken chair leg through the door handles in a hurried attempt to confine the Monster Bash bedlam.

"Uh, guys? Yay, hooray, big fuckin' reunion—*let's get out of here!*" he yelled as the doors began to rattle.

"Steve? I—" Julie started. Steve grinned madly, and shushed her with a finger pressed to her lips.

"I love you, too, hot stuff," he said. "Long time no see."

"*Guys!*" Stek grabbed Steve and wrenched him off Julie and into a standing position. "*Please!*"

Julie stood up slowly, her mouth working, her eyes darting about. Stek began jogging to the glass doors at the end of the corridor as the makeshift deadbolt began to crack.

Steve dusted himself off awkwardly before reaching out to help Julie up. She appeared to be shivering.

"Are you *crying?*" Steve said, his usual tone of mockery absent. "Hey, it's—"

Julie hugged him, fiercely, before pushing him away.

"Forget it, I guess," Stek called from the doors, throwing up his hands. "Just a typical fucking night. Don't worry about those fucking *werewolves* out there! Or the maniacs in the gym! We'll be *fine*—"

"Don't lose me," Julie said to Steve, and ran for the doors.

"Never again," Steve said, and followed her. The doors and the jack-o'-lantern lights out front seemed suddenly misty to him, almost as if there were tears in his *own* eyes. Gods forbid!

Julie was there. Right there in front of him. He saw her quite clearly, and now he knew he *had* been afraid.

But he wasn't anymore. *He could reach out and touch her.* The thought gave him tremendous courage.

WAKEFULNESS OBSCURED BY SLEEP; *sleep at first like the weight of rocks, then heaps of dirt, then dust, then nothing at all.*

Weston had *felt* something change, had delivered the unconscious girl in his trunk (the one wearing a sexy Catholic-schoolgirl outfit whom, alas, we know all too well—or perhaps not well enough) to the beasts at the edge of the forest as Yassiz had instructed. Their leader seemed somewhat perturbed that Weston had merely lit a cigarette in response to its growls and barks of acknowledgment, then bounded off with its fellows, howling madly on their merry way past the Lots-a-Burger and carrying the girl to her all-too-predictable fate on the roof of Honorius High.

Each moment utterly unconnected to any previous or future moments, except in the strange dream called "this life." It forms a narrative. A narrative gives the illusion of contents strung together with a particular meaningful connection...names are one. Attitudes and actions associated with those names are another. The limitation of the name and its "meaning" to the world creates the self that suffers, the self that is born and dies.

These thoughts—more like memories. Things he had thought before...right on the verge of waking from something...

He wandered into the Monster Ball without being noticed. He slipped past the smashing crowds without being touched. He found a mirror—and it all, quite suddenly, came back to him.

Some call this "good" and some call it "evil." Some do not care. Some wish it was all otherwise.

All these entities suffer from the limitation of their meanings, and they have enclosed those meanings in the envelope of their skin.

With this in mind, Yassiz had decided to play a game with the multiverse, given Its nature to REMEMBER and to COMPLETE—to *perfect*. In the midst of Its first perfection, the Laughing God had smiled to Itself and Realized a Means of Escape: *there was another option.*

"Another option" implied that failure to exercise it to its fullest extent would be failure to *complete*, failure to *perfect*— implied that Its "fellow" gods were, despite their rock-solid status as the cores of planets and stars and black holes, on most occasions, *failures.*

There is always *another option. Perfection implies an encapsulation of time.*

The Laughing God was like a package with a bomb inside: the bomb, of course, looked identical to what had been ordered...and you had *no idea*—Yassiz Itself had *no idea*—when the thing would go off, or even *if* it would...

It *remembered* Itself...*the false history, the false identity, the costume It had assumed to play the part of Weston Gray... And so* clever! *No chance It could've gotten past Laban's intricate magical defenses at the Flowers residence if It had retained any real belief in Its true identity...*

Sometimes, Yassiz astonished even Itself. There was still

work to be done, but now, *now*, It had a *plan*, It knew *just how to proceed...*

It did what It was known for, what always happened when It awoke from these self-induced dream-plays: Yassiz laughed.

It barely noticed the boy—*Charles Thomas Leland*—burst into the room. *But It knew why he was there...*

EDDIE VAN HALEN HAD reared back to avoid the swipe of Charley's sudden stroke of luck, but that is not what saved our intrepid hero. When Charley opened his eyes he saw, to his astonishment, a wide, axe-hewn swath of wall beside him missing, letting in a draft of cool spring air and a taste of freedom.

The taste, like filet mignon, was a memory shortly, as Charley shot through the man-sized tear in the fabric of school to a non-fatal escape. The axe had to be dropped in order to do so—but the purpose of weapons (even cool, magical ones) was to ensure one's life, after all, not put it into question. Eddie van Halen's arm followed him, but though an angry cracking sound vouched for Eddie's sincerity and threatened to cave the innards of the wall, Charley found himself sprinting with abandon beside the track field, unpursued save by howls of frustration from one of the greatest rock guitarists of all time.

Charley only slowed once, briefly, as he rounded the outer wall of the school, heading now for the front parking lot where, presumably, Julie and Stek sat by the DeLorean Time Machine, awaiting him and Steve—and Charley's brief mental wince at the thought of Steve's possible fate was quickly eclipsed by the reality of Steve's indomitable resolve, luck, and the general insistence by the multiverse that it preferred slight irritations to any other form of life.

FLOWERS DEVELOPMENT COMPANY HAD put a sign up on the doors of the old, abandoned Church of St. Bruno across the street from Honorius, claiming its imminent fate as a "recreational area for Golem Creek youth." The sign had quite a bit of rust on it, but its writing could be discerned, despite its age.

Julie was frantic. "*Where's Charley?*"

She paced in front of the DeLorean sitting in the parking lot of the church, right next to her Honda—the one she was still unsure whether she'd "borrowed" from herself or not here, in *this* Golem Creek, after Charley had arrived in a flash of time-traveling lightning.

Whatever had happened inside Honorius High, it appeared to be limited in its scope: only *some* of the student population had been possessed by the shadowy inhabitants of the Murk, and the creatures seemed loath to wander far from their teen-aged buffet.

Steve's eyes had been riveted to the DeLorean since he'd first approached it. He waved a hand toward Honorius, out of which screaming students occasionally ran, limped, or were flung. "I'm *sorry*, Jules! What do you want me to *do*? You haven't even explained where you've *been*—"

"Tulsa," Julie said flatly.

Steve was momentarily speechless. "Okay," he said. "Tulsa. So that's where your portal led?"

"Yeah," she answered. "In a sense."

Steve looked at her and reached out for a cigarette. "You owe me a cigarette. *And* an explanation." He pointed at Stek, who was running his hands over the DeLorean's stainless-steel roof.

"I don't owe you *shit*," Julie said. "I've spent the last... goddamnit, I can hardly *remember*! Six months? Almost a year? Living in Tulsa. *Going to grad school*."

Steve coughed. "*Grad* school? What the hell did you do *that* for?"

"Because that's what I was *doing* when I showed *up* there!"

Steve was silent for a moment. "Oh," he said. "I see."

Stek retreated behind the wheel of the DeLorean, gazing with sympathy at Steve, who leaned against the hood while Julie yelled at him.

It's an okay car, Stek thought, admiring the astonishingly accurate *Back to the Future* interior. *Not very roomy. Cramped. Even more room in Julie's fucking Civic.* A stab of anxiety suddenly ran through him. *Holy shit—does this one have a goddamned plutonium chamber...?*

"Well," Steve continued. "Was it fun?"

Julie struggled to light another cigarette. "Dude! We've got to go back *in* there and—"

"Hark!" Steve shouted, standing up sharply and pointing.

Charley came racing around the corner at one end of the school, heading straight for them and looking all-too-typical (i.e., as if pursued by some unnameable horror).

"Chuck!" Steve yelled as Charley shot across the street. "I was just telling Julie—"

"Get in the *car*!" Charley exclaimed breathlessly.

"We can't all fit in there—"

Charley practically slammed into the driver's side of the DeLorean. "Let me drive!" he shouted, wrenching Stek out of the seat.

"Well, all *right*, dude, I—"

"Guys! Seriously!" he said, turning the ignition. "*Get in*!"

"You just pulled me *out*—"

"Well get in Julie's car and try to keep up!" Charley was already closing the door.

Julie hopped into her Civic, followed by Stek.

Steve wasn't about to pass up a chance to ride in the DeLorean—not to mention a chance to let Julie cool off. They peeled out of the church parking lot, barely avoiding a loping, shambling *thing* crossing the road from the school, carrying two lumps that looked a lot like Honorius High staff.

"Is that Jim the Janitor?" Steve asked as they whizzed by. "Who's the other guy?"

Charley ignored him and floored the accelerator. "Too bad Wise didn't modify the engine on this thing," he said. "Marty could *never* have made it to eighty-eight in that parking lot."

"What?" Steve asked. He shook his head. "I admit that I'm baffled. Why did Mr. Fandolini let you take his car?"

"He didn't," Charley said.

Steve let out a sudden whoop of laughter and punched the roof. "Dude! Chuckie! I didn't think you had it *in* you, man! *Grand theft auto*?"

"Not quite," Charley said. "This car wasn't Mr. Fandolini's, because that wasn't Mr. Fandolini we saw earlier."

"All right," Steve said, rummaging through the glove compartment. "I'm listening." He extracted a half-empty pack of Camels. "Success!"

"There's a *lot* you don't know," Charley said.

"I'm beginning to become aware of that," Steve said. "Does it have to do with Roland? Did you find him again?"

"Kind of," Charley said. "Listen. I'm going to have to make this quick, because we've got at least one, ah, *thing* hot on our trail."

Steve looked over at Charley. "Okay. Go on. This is fucking gold, man."

"I've been gone for just over a year," Charley said.

"We've *both* been gone for at *least* a year—"

"No, no, you don't understand. Since you ran off to the Courtyard for a cigarette earlier tonight."

Steve looked straight ahead again. They had slowed to a stop by an automated car wash station. He glanced in the side-view mirror and saw both Julie's car edging up behind them and—with less enthusiasm than he would have felt before the Bhairavi Society had inaugurated—that fires had broken out in the vicinity of Honorius.

"What the *fuck* happened, man?"

"I may have figured out—or been shown—the *very root* of what's going on."

"And that is?"

"*Encephala*. You know—like, brains." Charley breathed out heavily in frustration, accelerating through the light as it turned green. "Functionally, at least. Maybe one brain?"

Steve nodded his head. "This makes absolutely perfect sense."

"It does?"

"Of *course* it doesn't, dude!" Steve shouted. " 'Brains.' What the fuck am I supposed to make of *that*? And *where the hell did this DeLorean come from*?"

"Wise Nerds," Charley answered.

"Fuck you, too," Steve said.

Charley was briefly taken aback. "No! No, I mean it! *Wise Nerds*. Doctor Wise Nerds! The guy."

Steve was shaking his head. "Never heard of him."

"I know!" Charley said. "I know. Neither had I! But then I made a *wish* the night of the Monster Ball—er, *tonight*, I mean, but a year ago. For me. And you had gone to get a smoke. You were going to the Courtyard. I reached in my pocket and found these keys." He tapped the keys hanging out of the ignition switch.

"And you were suddenly the proud owner of a—wait a second. *You made a* wish? Just like that?"

Charley was nodding his head excitedly. "Yes!"

"So we can time travel in this thing?" Steve asked.

"Absolutely!"

"Then why the *fuck* did you decide to come back *now* instead of, oh, I don't know, yesterday? Two days ago?"

Charley's grin melted away. "Yeah, well. Neither of us existed *in common* yesterday."

Steve looked at Charley wordlessly for a moment. "Okay. *Go on.*"

"It's not that crazy," Charley continued. "Wherever you are, from that point in spacetime, your wave function has adapted to the 'fact' of your environment. Typically, you take it for granted—like in a dream. You just go about your business with the assumption that your context is basically what it always has been, and will continue basically the way it always has, for the most part. So if I had come back *too soon, much* earlier than the time I left, I would have started bifurcating the universe I was trying to get back to *before I got back to it.*"

Steve nodded his head. "All right. Bullshit accepted." He sank back in the passenger seat. "Why is it that all a person has to do is make stuff just a *little* more complicated than it needs to be in order to get everybody to believe it?"

"I don't know," Charley said. "Ask Wise. He's the one who explained it to me."

Steve glanced around the dark streets. "*Where* are we going?"

"Brake Street," Charley answered. "We're going back to Mike's. I think I know what we're supposed to do."

"Okay," Steve said. "Now back to this *wish-making* thing—"

"Don't you remember? *We freed the genie*—we freed Roland from Laban's spell! And he gave us three wishes! But then we *forgot* about them when we made the switch here to Golem Creek from the Place of Solace—"

"I wish for an infinite number of wishes," Steve said immediately. He looked around. "Now I wish for a Nat Sherman cigarette."

Nothing happened.

"Why didn't it work?" he asked, a look of genuine perplexity on his face.

"You already used up your wish," Charley said.

"*What?*" Steve shouted. "Lies! What confounded farking foolishness—"

"You used your wish *earlier*—before we rearrived. It's part of the reason I'm back!"

Steve paused momentarily. "What did I wish for?" he asked anxiously.

Charley shook his head. "Doesn't matter. Look, we—"

"*What was it?*" Steve shouted, gripping his hair in both hands. "Tell me!"

Charley told him.

Steve slumped over and put his head in his hands.

"Steve?" Charley said with concern. "You all right, bud?"

A low chuckle answered his query.

"Gods be praised!" Steve shouted suddenly, raising his fists and eyes in triumph. "I was no fool! Yet I don't really remember this," he added. "I don't remember 'freeing Roland,' or whatever. *The last thing I remember—the earliest thing—is eating a Triple Decker at Lots-a-Burger.*" He looked at Charley. "Why can't I remember anything before that?"

"I'm sorry to have to tell you this," Charley said, "but it's because *nothing happened* before that. It'll change. It'll update. But it couldn't until I got back."

They pulled into Michael Flowers's old neighborhood and headed for Brake Street.

"I have only one further question for you," Steve said, a note of deep seriousness in his voice. "*Where is it?* Where is my greatest accomplishment?"

Charley shook his head. "I have no fucking idea."

Steve moaned and punched the roof. "I *will* find it! I must!"

"I'M SORRY, DUDE. REALLY, seriously, I am."

Jim the Janitor had been apologizing to Bax Laird since the troll or super-goblin or whatever-the-hell-it-was had kidnapped them half an hour ago.

Bax had remained silent until this moment.

"Listen, Jim," he said, leaning back on the concrete floor of the basement of St. Bruno's. "Just—go—fuck yourself. Okay? And maybe shut the hell up while you're at it."

Jim shut the hell up.

The creature had smashed its way into the church across from Honorius, using its own head as a battering ram, descended a series of ancient stone steps hidden behind the apse (also revealed via smashing), and, apparently quite certain of its hostages' lack of initiative, turned and loped out after unceremoniously dropping them on the cold, dark floor of the cold, dark room.

Jim had said it would be easy. He said that the girl— "Molly"—would be "delivered" to them, that all they'd need to do was take a quick jaunt back to Tulsa and drop her off with PyGoLiRo... Why had Bax thought it would be so easy?

"Gentlemen."

The voice emanated from the deep shadows at one end of the room.

"Your Majesty?" Jim spoke hesitantly, gathering himself up only to bow unctuously. Bax only gazed in the direction of the voice and shivered.

A chuckle sounded, laughter like bricks shattering in groups at the bottom of a canyon. "You get the prize for etiquette," the voice assured Jim, as its carrier stepped out of the shadows. "What name did I give you last? Hm. *Welcher Name paßt am besten zu mir?*"

Bax looked over at Jim, whose servile demeanor had more than a touch of fear to it. The entity looked like a devil, to be sure: a classic devil with wicked horns and reptilian features. The immaculate black tuxedo with the blood-red rose in its lapel added an even more classic touch: *the Devil, Satan, the Salesman, the Gambler...*

"Fuck it," the Devil said. "Call me Yassiz." He pronounced it *YAH-seez.* "Or Weston. Either one. And I apologize for the rough handling by Jorgensen."

Bax grinned nervously. "You're—*you're* the Laughing God?" He turned to Jim for confirmation, who still stood with his head bowed. He turned back. "That thing's name is *Jorgensen?*" he said, incredulous.

Yassiz grinned. "Hey, *I'm* not his fucking parents," he said. Suddenly, his grin disappeared. "I don't think," he added.

Yassiz shook his head. "Anyway, like I said, sorry about the strained lines of communication, et cetera, et cetera." He sat down in a throne that was suddenly right behind him. Spotlights shone on it from some invisible source in the room. "Let's get down to business! But first—first—maybe you guys could do me a favor?"

Bax noticed that large sweat marks had appeared through Jim's janitorial jumpsuit.

"Great! I'll take silence as a definitive 'yes' over a 'no' any day!" Yassiz bent over, laughing hysterically. "Plus, I don't even know how many people I had to eviscerate to get here. Two more would just be *excessive!*"

Jim decided to chance a suggestive comment. "Anything required by the noble PyGoLiRo—*ahh!*"

Bax heard the audible snap of bone as Jim collapsed to the floor, gripping his right knee in both hands and shrieking in pain.

"Did you—*did you just*—" Yassiz stood from his throne, which suddenly appeared constructed of human skulls and black iron. He pointed an accusatory, razor-sharp fingernail at Jim. "*Did you just say 'noble'?*"

Tears covered Jim's face, his eyes held by Yassiz, his throat choked with terror. "I did—I did *not know*—"

Bax heard another sharp snap, followed by a scream, then gasping breaths. Jim felt his leg for the break, which *had* been there—in its place, nothing but smooth flesh, uncompromised.

"Right! Right. Sorry, again. Sometimes I mishear things." Yassiz sighed and slumped back in his (now royal crimson and griffin-skin) throne. "It's my age, I think. I feel like I'm a billion years old, these days. *Anyway*"—he took a few puffs off a gigantic cigar that had just materialized—"I need you guys to go grab that chick for me. Marigold?" He blew out smoke, gazing with consternation at it as the cloud formed a bouquet of flowers. "No. That's not it." He flicked his eyes over at Bax, who winced. "It's *Molly*. That's her. That's my girl!"

The coldness Bax had felt in his chest penetrated him further. *Oh, Christ, we're in for it now...*

"Yes, of course," Jim said. Bax shook his head. *Doesn't that guy ever learn? 'Don't speak unless spoken to'—that's a pretty basic axiom with crazy magical creatures.* "It's Molly Furnival you're looking for. But—"

He had been about to say, *I thought you wanted her delivered to PYGOLIRO tonight.*

"But?" Yassiz asked, raising the thin, scaly lines of his eyebrows. "But what? *You were about to say something?*"

"Ah, yes, of course, *but* is there anything *else* you'd like us to do for you?" Jim breathed out. He started coughing.

"How kind of you to offer!" Yassiz shouted. "Sure. I'm sure I'll think of *something*! But it's pretty important that you get her for me. I'll need you to get her back to Mr. Black's for the final process." He paused, gazing upward. "Oh. You'll need something—some means of restraining her." A few tense seconds elapsed before he snapped his "fingers." "Perfect! Lucky me! Someone's already provided a simple solution!" He stared at them, sending waves of sheer terror through Bax. "Well? Get going! *Now*, please!"

Yassiz waved goodbye dramatically. Jim and Bax disappeared.

"OH, MAN! I HAVEN'T been back here in *forever*!" Steve shook the door handle at the old Bhairavi Society Headquarters behind the abandoned Flowers family residence. "Locked. Damn it." He banged loudly on the door with the flat of his hand twice.

"Knock it off, dude," Charley said. "We're not going in there."

"What?" Steve looked hurt.

"We're going to the basement of the main house," Julie said.

Stek was already rattling the chain on the cellar doors at the back of the house. "Anyone got a key?" he said, chuckling.

"Yeah," Charley responded. "Hang on. Let me see."

In short order, the four of them were heading down the cellar stairs. Steve closed the doors behind them.

) ★ (

"WHAT IN THE GODDAMN-BLOODY-HELL is going on?" Charley asked as the scene shifted dramatically.

They were in a large, basically empty (as far as they could tell), stadium-seating movie theater. Each of the four blown minds sat in their own capitalist variant of a king's throne: a soft, well-upholstered easy chair. Wise Nerds reclined in their midst, enthusiastically shoveling handfuls of popcorn into his mouth.

"Mechanics!" he shouted for no apparent reason. They gazed at him, speechless, prepared for nearly anything.

Wise cleared his throat. "Attend!" he shouted.

He waved a hand and complicated schematics sprang out of nowhere against the screen. Charley glanced at Wise, confused, before lifting his hands in despair. "Wise! What in the *world* is this all about?"

"Um," Steve attempted. "Does anyone else—um. What should I ask? Who is this guy?"

Stek stood up and sat down repeatedly, frowning as he attempted to determine the relative materiality of his seat.

"Okay, sure. Portals. Parallel worlds," Julie said. "But how is this even *possibly* making any sense, much less *happening at all*?" She gripped both sides of her head and closed her eyes.

"Forget it," Wise said. "Let's try something a little easier.

And may I request—*silence during the proceedings!*"

The four reality-abductees fell silent in consternation as the theater darkened.

"This should be sufficient," Wise Nerds said. He turned to regard a small window of light far above and behind them. "Projectionist! On with the show!"

"Have some!" Wise Nerds insisted, grinning broadly as he handed Charley his tub of popcorn. A humanoid pig wearing a chef's hat was emblazoned on the yellow-and-orange-striped side of it.

A ratings screen appeared before them.

A	AWESOME	THEMATIC ELEMENTS INVOLVING TEEN DRUG USE, GRAPHIC VIOLENCE, AND SEQUENCES OF NIGHTMARISH MONSTER PARTIES

The popcorn, they were pleased to discover, was deliciously buttery, and salted with an addictive, almost stuffing-flavored spice. Charley dropped a single popped kernel. An enterprising mouse appeared from beneath one of the seats, grabbed it, and skittered off.

The show started.

"C'mon, baby! It'll only take a _minute_!"

The blond jock sported a varsity football jacket with the letters "GC" emblazoned on it in classic, jersey-letter font. The cheerleader with him was half-drunk, half-stoned, and lazily fighting off his advances.

They were in a graveyard — the Foxend Churchyard, to be precise. A horned moon rose in the distance above Chicken Hill. It could be dimly spotted between the dark branches of the oak tree beneath which unfolded our After-School Special.

"Marco! _No_!" The cheerleader pushed mightily against the bulk of Marco's chest. She knew that

scolding him like a bad dog had an uncanny knack of
actually getting him to lay off.

Marco laid off and stood up, backing away a few
paces and sulking. "This isn't fair!" he shouted to the
sky, to the entombed dead surrounding him. "Jenny! Why
would you do this to me?"

He never saw what tore through him at that moment.
Parts of Marco littered the ground seconds later.

[Cascades of elegant gore form a Jackson Pollock on
the screen.]

"Cool effect," Charley commented. He sensed Wise Nerds
nodding vigorously in the chair beside him.

The girl whimpered as the beast that had ended
Marco turned its attention to her. She noted that it
appeared to be <u>chewing</u> — crunching an unidentifiable
hunk of Marco's carcass.

What, indeed was the thing? Every folk story and
urban legend she'd ever heard blackened her memory
as she attempted to cope with its monstrosity. A
shroud of darkness beset with a large, cumbersome
head, jagged teeth, long, razor-sharp claws on spindly
fingers...

<u>It can't be</u>... she thought desperately. "It can't be
<u>you</u>! You don't <u>exist</u>!"

[A dark shape rises up before the camera, and we
(the audience) descend upon her, our gore-bespattered
maw rupturing her jugular vein.]

[All goes silent as the camera cuts to a shot of
the dark woods at the edge of the graveyard — nothing
is heard but crickets.]

"Those crickets are in the theater," Wise Nerds whispered.
He handed Charley a Mega-Sized Cherry Coke.

The camera panned out and up to display the World—or,
at least, Golem Creek. Surrounding the city shone a hazy mist,
shimmering, a hint of small creatures flittering about within

it. The surrounding mist faded into an indigo darkness within which appeared occasional fulgurations.

"Probability waves," Wise Nerds commented, reading Steve's mind.

And they descended once again, by way of the wild, flaming bacchanal that was Honorius High School, back to Brake Street.

))★((

"OKAY, OKAY," JIM SAID as he and Bax re-appeared suddenly elsewhere, "I think I know what to do."

It was a toy store—but how to convey the miracle that was—

"Steve's Endless Warehouse of Every Toy & Game Imaginable?" Bax read aloud from a discarded box top. He began inspecting shelves, of which there were hundreds, thousands, ranged above, below, behind, and ahead of him. Dim, flickering fluorescent lighting ran in tracks along the ceiling. The shelves were of yellowing off-white aluminum. Their ordinary make only enhanced the extraordinary merchandise on display.

Jim had trudged ahead to the end of the aisle. "I think..." He trailed off, holding a finger to his lips. "This way?" He headed off to the left.

Bax Laird, dazed and confused (yes, exactly like that), turned briefly to watch Jim disappear around a corner. He was unsure of what precisely to say, given as he felt utterly unsure of what precisely the fuck was going on.

"Jim?" he finally attempted. "Hey, Jim! Where the hell are we?"

Aside from some shuffling a few aisles over and the sound of boxes falling from a decent height, there was no answer. Bax returned his gaze to the shelf in front of him: neatly arranged, in their original packaging, hundreds of Monsters in my Pocket™ gazed back at him. He lifted up a red "Werewolf," howling in wicked glee. *25 points!* the package proclaimed triumphantly.

Bax felt a quiet elation well up within him. *Maybe I could just hide out here? Occupy myself cataloging this place?* He sighed, but tried to maintain a degree of satisfaction. Certainly, it wasn't going to work out the way he wanted it to—with Jim, it never did. Exactly half the relevant information or less would be conveyed to Bax—as much or as little as he needed to know to further Jim's plans. Yes, Jim the Janitor, Eternal Enemy of "You-Name-It" Incorporated, and Sometime-Rewarded Servant of Yassiz, the Laughing God.

Jim's cool magical powers were convincing enough to keep Bax complacent for the time being—and the promises kept coming that Bax would get *something* awesome of his own soon. But things had certainly gotten *bloodier* than he'd expected.

This was the first time he'd ever been teleported to a magical toy warehouse, though, and that was pretty neat.

"Ah, to hell with it," he said, and allowed himself to smile. He began wandering through the aisles, delighting in the old sport of hunting for cool things. *I haven't done this in...gods, has it been THAT long?*

Boxes of unpacked merchandise were stacked along what appeared to be a back wall. He opened one up at random. A Boglin stared back at him from its cardboard-and-plastic cage.

Bax grinned. He thought he could discern a tiny red "EXIT" sign many leagues away. The place was muffled and close, packed to the brim with every possible item he could imagine or remember. He turned back after reaching the garish pink hues of a "girls' section" sporting Barbies, Jem dolls, Cabbage Patch kids, Easy-Bake Ovens, fake jewelry, and hundreds of nameless, sleepy-eyed stuffed animals and dolls.

Some distance from where he *thought* they'd arrived, he discovered an oasis of old science hobby kits: chemistry sets in basic, elementary, intermediate, advanced, and super-advanced (this last had a kid on the front of it marveling at a grand explosion), rows and rows of carefully labeled and organized chemicals, electronics kits (also in basic-through-mega-advanced versions), ham and crystal radio sets, toy rockets, microscopes, telescopes (one of which occupied its own mini-observatory), then on to dissection kits, racks and racks of manuals on how to build/do/see/discover damn-near-any-thing (many by the dimly remembered Information Unlimited, whose "Ion-Ray Gun" Bax had faithfully ordered the blueprints of, though he had failed to construct it, unaware of how to obtain a "zener diode")...ah, and here we come across a vast hall of Sea Monkey Aquaria, along with the entire catalog of itemry (Bax paused to marvel at the famed "Teach Your Sea Monkeys to Play Baseball!" equipment)...

Bax became finally convinced of the warehouse's veritable claim of endlessness when, to his extraordinary delight, he beheld the complete set of viscoelastic urethane polymer Manglors™ action figures and accessories, neatly displayed along one dimly lit aisle—a prodigy of juvenescent artifice.

He actually found himself *rushing* to the spooky glow of what appeared to be a fully bedecked Halloween costume section when a sudden sensation made him pause.

How long had he been here? Where the hell was Jim? And, perhaps most importantly, how could he locate this genius "Steve" and beg him for a job?!?

CHAPTER I

A NIGHTMARE ON
BRAKE STREET

WANDERING THROUGH THE PLACE of Solace.

Carven with such care, such painstaking artistry, you will note the great Sphinxes and Chimæras here flanking the entrance to Candleston Manor, several leagues distant from the Pyramid of Laban Black. There are seventy-eight of them; thirty-nine to a side, each one exquisitely shaped to represent a Principle of the Universe.

The road itself is macadam, and the flowers and herbs that adorn the pedestals of each sculpture (which appear to be impossibly constructed out of a fine marble stone) possess unique affiliations with the Principle they announce.

Great beds of roses, the deepest scarlet imaginable, with petals delicate and velutinous as the dawn, rise out of waters blue and unquenchable surrounding the Færy Fountain, where wishes are granted when the right coin is drowned within its unfathomable depths. You may feel overwhelmed, saturated with enchantment by the dazzling array; *vide quid agas!* A *cacoëthes* compels you to stay, but resist! Candleston Manor lies ahead.

You may proceed left or right around the Fountain.

Reaching the steps of the Manor, please note the fine gold trim of the gas lamps, embroidered with the images of Guardian Spirits, grinning each, as they know you cannot pass if you are not an illusion. The fire flickers into life within; the crystal windows of the lamps echo with many flames, all one.

Taking the steps by way of a maroon runner that remains

169

dry through any season, we count twelve of them. A hidden thirteenth step may sometimes appear on Great Nights—this, they say, leads to a different castle with different miracles.

Tonight, alas, we arrive at the entrance of Candleston Manor. A wood fire has been stoked somewhere near, as a piercing wind begins, the passage of a small winter in a great world. It may be gone in the morning, as there is no lord of the manor (this we all know), only the wishes of those who abide within.

AND JUST PAST THE entryway, that oak monstrosity, we scuttle quickly through the foyer, past the split staircase, the stone busts of unknown celebrities in niches (with hidden panels behind—but we skip that for now), through the barely discernible little door hidden in shadow to the right of the main hallway (although the smells of a gluttonous feast waft teasingly, beckoning from the kitchens beyond). We just barely squeeze into a little, yellow-lit, helical staircase that winds downward.

That's a portrait of Master Curwen—could be some goblin thought it might raise a few laughs, especially with what must be an offering plate set beneath it. Gibbous candlelight illuminates the way, though it seems always dark just ahead.

Not a coincidence.

To the alcove, at last! Must be at least two stories beneath the Manor proper. And a window here! Tho' we headed *down*, it looks out at starlit night and the tops of massive dark woods, swaying gently in a low, chilly breeze.

There, at the other end of the room, with the oil lamp sputtering above it. Turn the knob; bare the wick. That's it.

Not just any book sits on that lectern. Yes, it appears to be some sort of elegant encyclopedia—the writing is dreadfully small, practically microscopic. Some reading glasses ought to help—here, hooked to the edge of the lectern.

The characters in our story thought they were alone that night, but there was Someone watching, unbidden...

"THE PRINCE OF DARKNESS is a Flame."

A voice, cool and relaxed, speaks from everywhere at once. It sounds almost as if it is reading.

"That which is royal *rules over* its domain. The Prince of Darkness is, thus, clearly Fire and Flame—that which rules Darkness. But we already knew this by way of the legend of Lucifer. Various *keys*"—the word is emphasized, as if to indicate something within it—"occur throughout the mythologies. That is, throughout our various *histories*."

You walk, relaxed and assured, down a hallway. The room with the book is gone, but the voice continues to emanate. On either side of the hallway, reminding you of the effect made when facing two mirrors to one another, are doors...the hall seems to bend and diminish ahead as you continue...

"An *eye* and a *hand* guide you. A bolt of lightning shimmering in darkness. *The ancient rites of Summanus*, the dark form of Io-Pater, and the 'one as many' in a hymn to the Panic God—"

A door slams somewhere behind you, and you pick up your pace. Something is following you.

"—don't forget! Remember! Seven stars in the North; *vinum sabbati*; infinite *kosmoi* running in parallel with the one you are focusing and projecting *now*—"

Footsteps coming closer—*something is behind you*—

"And now—now for *the point*—"

HOW THE INFORMATION HAD come to be in his mind—how *precisely* he knew *where* he was and *what* he was to look for—Jim supposed to be simply the miraculous working of Lord Yassiz, the limitations of Whose Powers he had yet to imagine.

Jim felt himself drawn forward, toward a majestic display of Pez dispensers, then left, past racks of Star Wars figurines and TIE fighters (offset, of course, by Spock and Kirk and Captain Picard and Lieutenant Data, directly across the hall), to be met with a most peculiar phenomenon: an upturned beetle, approximately a foot long, kicking its spindly legs pathetically in a futile attempt to right itself.

Jim knelt down and gazed at it a moment before boldly grasping one of its furry legs and angling it upright.

The creature paused for a moment, shook briefly from *cephalos* to abdomen, then, with clear intention, lifted one foreleg in silent urging to its savior, and trotted off to the right.

Jim lost not a moment in contemplation of this wondrous event. He followed, obediently, past Michelangelo, Donatello, Leonardo, and Raphael bearing nunchaku, bo, katana, and sai (respectively), the Mad Scientist™ Glowing Glop, Monster Lab, and Dissect-an-Alien kits, stacks of Ray, Peter, Egon, Winston, and Slimer (admittedly, he paused once to admire the Ecto-1 in its pristine case), to arrive, ultimately, at one item hitherto unbeknownst to him (or to his world at large): the "Færy Queen Guillotine," mint condition in the box.

The beetle appeared to nod at him and salute with one foreleg before raising its variegated black elytra and fluttering off into the rafters, knocking once—twice—into a dim fluorescent bulb, then heading off for further unknown countries.

Jim hefted the box. It weighed about ten pounds, stood about three feet high, and was, indeed, what it proclaimed: a unique guillotine—*Fashioned of Færy-Proof Adamantium Steel!*— just large enough to fit around a human neck, but *Made for Teaching Those Pesky Færies a Lesson!*

It wasn't so much the guillotine that he needed, though. Jim instinctively looked right and left before pulling the tape off the top of the box and opening it, revealing—ah, yes! There it is!

Includes Færy-Proof Færy-Catching Noose & Magic-Resistant Pole!*

HALFWAY DOWN THE CONCRETE steps into the first cellar of the Flowers mansion, Steve paused and took a deep breath.

"Movie-theater popcorn?" he asked aloud. "Does anyone else smell that?"

---

* The fine print (which Jim in his sleep-deprived, partially hungover, hyper-adrenalized condition did *not* review) reads: "Up to 6 feet/1.83 meters. Not liable for damages incurred by other fey or magical creatures who may desire to free their captive friend. CYA at all times."

"I was *hoping* someone would say that!" Stek answered from the bottom of the stairs. "I totally do!"

"Guys, let's stay focused," Charley said. "There's no movie theater down here." He felt around the wall at the base of the stairs and pressed a round button. Seconds later, several dim bulbs gasped into life.

Julie sniffed twice. "It's like I was *eating* it, maybe. Just a minute ago."

"Are you *sure* there's no theater down here?" Steve said doubtfully as they made it into the dark cellar. "Because if Mike was holding out on us all that time, I'm gonna have Julie bring his ass back from the dead again so I can *beat him down*—"

"Again?" Stek interrupted, incredulous. "Did you say bring him back *again*?"

An angry howling accompanied by sounds of smashing metal and splintering glass arose like some infernal piece of performance art from the street outside.

"Oh, *no*..." Charley whispered, glancing up. "That *can't* be—"

"I'll be right back," Steve said, and sprinted over to the other side of the cellar, where steps led up into the house proper.

Stek tapped Charley on the shoulder. "Is he *always* doing stuff like that? Running straight into the jaws of death, I mean?"

Julie and Charley both nodded wordlessly.

"He'll be back," Charley said, shoving a large wooden crate away from part of the wall and revealing the outline of a door.

"He's part roach," Julie explained. "Possibly more roach than man. Nearly impossible to kill."

Charley chuckled as he felt along the top of the outlined door for a switch. "*Can* he be killed?" he asked.

"And speaking of all this death stuff, what was Steve saying about Mike Flowers?" Stek asked.

There was a click as Charley's hand found the catch. Charley grinned. The door collapsed inward a bit. It swung wide with a noisy creak as he pushed it, revealing more stone steps leading downward, miraculously lit by torches alongside a stone wall.

"I promise I'll explain it to you later," Charley said.

"What is this place?" Julie asked as they followed Charley down.

"It's Laban Black's old ritual chamber," he said. "It's where this whole business of the Murk really started."

"Why is it that scary magic chambers are always in deep, dark places?" Stek asked, flinching at grotesque shadows painted on the walls by torchlight. "Did I just answer my own question?"

"Oh, not all of them are," Charley said with unusual certainty. "If they're for infernal evocation, it's to ground the magician. Try doing that shit on a second or third floor and see what happens!"

"And where the hell did you learn that?" Julie asked, recalling a time when Charles Leland had known nothing whatsoever of dark magic.

Charley was silent as they exited into the chamber at the base of the curving stairs, which seemed to take up far more space than seemed possible. An eerie illumination, emanating from no discernible source, coupled with more torchlight along the walls to reveal flagstones painted with arcane symbols surrounding a brazier occupying the center of the room.

"Over there." Charley pointed to the far end of the room. "Do you see that spot on the ceiling, there?"

Julie crept a bit closer to the indicated area. Stek became briefly fascinated by the objects arranged on the ground surrounding the circle of evocation, and recoiled in silent horror when he realized that they were bones.

"Ah, Charley?" he said. "You *are* aware that this is very probably a *murder site*?"

Charley nodded. "Not just one murder, either," he said. Stek shivered visibly.

On the other side of the circle, Julie approached a triangle that had been painted on the floor. She looked up to see an identical triangle on the ceiling, a mirror image of the one on the floor, but made of some reflective black substance, like polished obsidian.

"Wait a minute," she said. "This triangle—this must be *right underneath*—"

"The Bhairavi Society meeting place," Charley finished for her. "Where the magical box with the key and the book from another world *linked up* and formed a makeshift portal to the Place of Solace."

"So what are we supposed to do here?" Julie asked.

Charley walked around the edge of the bone-circle to join her, pulling out the copy of *Fear Club* as he did so.

"The book?" Julie said. "The book you wrote. To find me."

Charley nodded. "By the gods am I glad you brought this back with you," he said. "Its purpose is complete. It's still tying us to that other world. And it seems to be causing some...problems." He paused and grinned. "Sorry about the title," he said, shrugging and placing the book in the center of the triangle inscribed on the floor. "Steve said it should've been something else."

Julie placed her hand on Charley's as he removed it from the book. "Thank you," she said.

Clattering from above indicated Steve's sudden reappearance in the cellar.

Charley grinned. "It was nothing! You would've done the same for me."

"So what're we supposed to d—"

They both turned to watch as Steve literally tumbled down the stairs into the room. Stek ran over to him.

"What the hell!" Stek said, helping him up. "Are you all right?"

Steve glanced around, looking slightly dazed, then grinned and took Stek's hand. "Sure," he said. "Sure thing! Thanks, bro."

Stek nearly lost his balance helping Steve up.

"What the hell happened up there?" Charley asked.

"Oh, Christ, man! Bad news," Steve said. "No more time machine."

"*What!*" Charley shouted.

"Well, that's what you get for leaving a marked vehicle out where any monster can find it," Steve said. "I'm sure we can fix it, right?"

Charley shook his head. "And *how* would we do that, genius?"

"I don't know—Stek, don't you have a car?"

"It's not a fucking *time machine*, dude!" Stek said.

"Well, this is just groovy," Charley said, turning back to the triangle. Julie knelt by the edge of it, gazing at the book wistfully. The scene on the cover appeared to be shimmering with a strange purple light. "That was kind of my getaway plan." He knelt next to her. "Man! The fucking *DeLorean*, of all *goddamned* things!"

Steve came jogging over and patted Charley on the back. "You worry too much, dude. If you can get *one* time machine, you can get *another*! Haven't you learned *anything*? Besides, the important thing is that Monster van Halen smashed your car because he seemed pissed off that he couldn't get in the house." Steve started laughing. "He even smashed his *guitar* on the curb outside before he went stomping off." He turned to Julie. "The Civic looks just like the vintage economy car it always was, by the way."

"Thanks for the update," Julie said. She pointed at the book. "Is this supposed to be doing something?"

Charley nodded. "Yeah, well," he said, still clearly upset. "You have the lighter?"

"What lighter?" Julie asked.

"The lighter. The one that Roland gave you."

"Christ! How do I keep forgetting these things?" she extracted the Soloviev Fabergé cigarette lighter from the inside pocket of her jean jacket and handed it to Charley. "I'm still getting used to the overlap you mentioned in the book. I keep thinking my grandmother gave me that thing when I was ten years old. She said it was lucky."

"You bet your ass it's lucky," Charley said, testing the flame. It ignited instantly. "The Fire of Fate. Each of the worlds tries to explain all of the others. Everything's being said in multiple ways, all at the same time. And this Fire destroys essential falsehoods."

Stek approached the other side of the triangle. They all gazed at the clean, reddish-orange flame in Charley's hands.

"Are you gonna burn it?" he asked.

Charley nodded. "It's the only way to free us," he said cryptically, and began to lower the lighter toward *Fear Club*.

"Wait!" Steve said. "Wait. Hang on. Classic moment."

He pulled out a cigarette, leaned over Charley's shoulder, and lit it on the Fire of Fate. Julie frowned. Charley hung his head briefly. Stek grinned.

"Okay," Steve said, breathing out smoke. "Okay, dude. Fire away."

"*Don't you fucking DARE!*"

The ragged voice came from the stairwell. A man stood there, brandishing some kind of dog-catcher's noose on a tele-scoping pole, at the end of which slumped the tired, frazzled, black-eyed form of Molly Furnival.

"*Molly?*" Charley said.

It was clearly her, though no form of Molly Furnival Charley or any of the others had ever seen. She appeared to be wearing a dress made of flowers, but most of it had been torn to shreds, revealing a muddy slip beneath. Her face was bruised and smudged with dirt; her hands, still instinctively angled elegantly at her sides, like those of a ballerina, shook slightly, the nails of her fingers chipped, her palms scuffed and bleeding.

"Get away from her, you bastard!" Stek shouted, moving hesitantly toward the intruder.

"I *knew* that was Jim the Janitor I saw before!" Steve announced gleefully, grinning despite himself.

Julie grabbed the lighter out of Charley's hand and dropped it on the book, which instantly shot up into a column of flame reaching the second triangle in the ceiling above.

Julie fell back from the flame alongside Charley and Steve.

"*NO!*" Jim shrieked, and attempted to leap toward the triangle through the circle. An invisible forcefield at the circle's edge knocked him back.

He lost his grip on Molly's noose.

Stek came at Jim from around the circle's edge. "You *sono-fabitch*," he yelled, lunging at Jim and punching him squarely in the jaw.

The janitor slumped to the flagstones, apparently out cold.

Shaking out his fist, Stek crept over to Molly, her once-perfect hair a frizzy mess covering her face, her unflappable elegance quite roundly flapped.

"Molly?" he said tentatively, reaching out to her.

As he was about to touch her, she shrieked and flung a hand at him. "Don't *look* at me! Get this damned thing off me!"

Stek cringed. *Still the same Molly Furnival.* "Whatever you say, dear," Stek said sarcastically. "But I'm going to have to look at you in order to get it off, you know..."

The column of flame within the triangle had dwindled, replaced by a pillar of smoke being sucked through the dark triangle on the ceiling above.

Charley, Steve, and Julie stood.

"I don't feel any different," Steve said, frowning. "Why don't I ever feel any different when magic shit happens?"

"'Cause that's just what magic is made out of," Charley explained. "Nothingness. Like everything else."

Steve looked briefly satisfied by the answer.

"What's going on with them?" Julie asked, nodding toward Stek gingerly trying to loosen the noose around Molly's neck.

"Don't know," Charley said. "More importantly—"

"Hey," Steve said, looking with consternation at the unconscious janitor. "What's the deal with that guy's hand?"

Charley noticed the mauve glow emanating from Jim's palm at roughly the same time Julie glanced back at the triangle, which had thoroughly cleared of smoke.

"Um, Charley?" she said nervously.

"I...don't know," Charley answered Steve. "Julie?" He turned back to her. "What's—"

Julie reached into the center of the triangle and lifted up a pristine copy of *Fear Club*. "Was that supposed to happen?" she asked. Her eyes narrowed briefly as she focused on the cover. "It doesn't say your name anymore. Who the hell is

'Damian Stephens'? And where's my *lighter*, after all that?"

Charley groaned. "I don't think this is good."

A wind began to pick up in the room.

"Dude, I don't like the looks of this," Steve said. "I suggest we get our asses back outside, van Halen monster or no."

They edged past Jim's prone form, toward the bottom of the stairs where Stek still sat fumbling with Molly's noose.

The glow brightened as they approached. The soft, swirling breeze in the room had evolved into a substantial wind that seemed to mean business.

"I think this has something to do with that glowing symbol in his palm," Steve said as he skipped up the first few stairs. "How about you?"

"Stek, we should go," Julie said, tapping him on the shoulder.

"What can we do to help?" Charley said, gazing down at Molly, who seemed to be trying to hide in plain sight.

Stek struggled with the clasp at the edge of the noose. "I don't know," he said. The wind had begun whipping through Molly's hair. She tried to hold the frazzled ends of it down over her face. "It seems to be stuck."

"Well, would it be too weird to just bring it along?" Charley suggested.

"Guys?" Steve peered around the edge of the staircase. "Looks like the janitor's ready to clean house. We should probably, you know, get the flying fuck out of here."

The bones encircling the floor began to vibrate, as did Jim's body, still apparently unconscious several feet away. The Mark of Yassiz on his palm glowed steadily now, outshining the torches on the walls, the flames of which flared out sideways in the breeze.

"Yeah, let's try this," Stek said. "Molly? Can we—"

She stood without speaking, head down, and waved them forward. Steve grinned and scampered up, out of sight.

"Go," she said. "I cannot."

"What?" Stek said. Charley and Julie paused at the foot of the stairs.

"He is binding me here," she responded, indicating Jim

with one dirt-encrusted hand. "You must go, or you will be consumed as well."

"*Consumed*?" Stek said, stepping back toward her.

Molly held out her hand to fend him off. "*Go*," she said, summoning every ounce of queenly deportment she had left.

Stek looked back at Charley and Julie, who both stood at the foot of the stairs.

"There's got to be *something*—" he started.

"There is," Charley said, raising his voice as the wind began rushing through the chamber. He turned to Julie. "Wish for it."

Julie stared back at him. "What?"

"*Wish for it*!" Charley insisted. "You haven't used your wish yet! *Do it*!"

"Wish? What are you talking ab—"

"*Just say it*!" Charley yelled as Jim's body in its entirety began shimmering with radiant mauve light.

"Fine! *I wish that Molly Furnival was perfectly safe from all harm.* There! Are you satisfied?"

A brief blast of radiant white light consumed the room, blinding everyone.

The wind ceased abruptly. When they uncovered their eyes, Molly was gone, the pole and noose clattering to the floor.

"Guys!" Steve's voice came from the top of the stairwell. "Are you dead yet? What the fuck was that?"

"*You DARE interfere with HIS WORK?!*"

Jim the Janitor levitated several feet off the floor, his body glowing, his face a semblance of demonic fury.

Stek flung himself toward the stairs with a girlish shriek, a single beat behind Charley and Julie, who stumbled over themselves on their way up.

"*You will be PUNISHED for this!!! AVAVAGO!*"

Again, the winds, a tornado of devilish fire; a moment of ecstasy; and Jim the Janitor descended slowly to the floor of a quiet, empty room, the only living inhabitant of the Flowers mansion.

IT WAS THE DARKEST hour of Walpurgisnacht. You could hear them now, all the terrors of the Murk in frenzied cacophony, bursting forth from Honorius, surging into the streets, wildly fulfilling their promise of a long-awaited vengeance on Golem Creek.

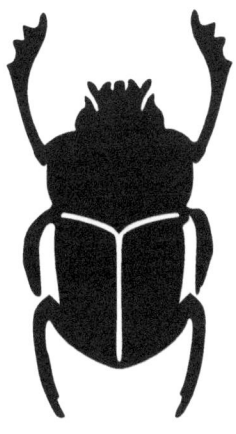

From the Notebooks of
Michael Flowers

~~~ The Formula of Unhingement ~~~

the shapes you must use
in blood drawn
and the abomination of desolation
by great moonlight discover'd

Places haunted by continual darkness or wild beasts—these are acceptable. Whatever invokes great fear, whatever dispels tranquility—these are the sacraments.

As the moon darkens, withdraw from the world of men.

Let sleep come as it will—remove all means and methods of time-keeping. Where we traverse, civilization has never been.

When the disparity between waking and sleeping has been conquered, begin the Rite.

Call Yog Sothoth by his several names; arrange the Stones if the Rite occurs in some unhallowed place.

Call to the Eight Directions. When the crack in the worlds appears, let the Cloud be formulated.

You will be taken thereby past the Pylons of Chaos. Here, you must divest yourself of those human parts still clinging to your True Self. (This is why the Rite is of great danger to novices; the Wizards of the past often simply used this Method to destroy unwanted candidates.)

When Choronzon has finished with you, then the Unhingement. This will appear to you as Seven Great Stars behind which lieth a deep and unfathomable blackness.

The Jewel will fall therefrom. If your presence is still required in the material realm, you will be returned.

NOTE: *To avoid capture,* dive through the Cone.

EPILOGUE

☽ ★ ☾

MADDER MUSIC
&
STRONGER WINE!

FROM AN INTERVIEW WITH *Nashe St.-Demp* [sic] *by Merlin Tuttle in* Isaac Asthma's Nonstandard Science Magazine, *Volume LXVI, Issue 13, Pp. 78-80:*

Merlin Tuttle: When did you decide to write under the pseudonym "Damian Stephens"?

Damian Stephens: [laughs] It was a matter of personal safety! [sips a glowing purplish liquid from an unlabeled Mason jar] Really. Seriously.

MT: Why write at all, then?

DS: I had to do something! I mean, those kids were in deep shit, you know? And there's only a few methods I know of for contacting parallel universes—the easiest is just to send a story out. Get it published. That automatically alerts the Old Ones, which jars the gates somewhat. [pauses] I mean, if it ain't just some Danielle Steel or Tom Clancy bullshit.

MT: When did Golem Creek become an important aspect of your writing?

DS: I started having strange dreams about a city of that name in my late teens. I talked to a good friend of mine about it, but I acted like I made the stuff up—I put most of it in short story form. I'd go over to his place and we'd get drunk on a mini-keg of Warsteiner beer and smoke a ton of cigarettes and I'd read him the "episodes" I'd written.

MT: What did he think of the ideas?

DS: He liked some of it. Other parts he thought could be better. The usual. [pulls out what is obviously a marijuana cigarette and proceeds to spark it] Oh. Do you mind?

MT: Only if you don't give me some!

DS: [laughs] I don't know if you can handle this shit. This is the Doobis, man—Doobis Anubis! Get it? [laughs]

MT: Right. Funny. Anyway, you said that you started dreaming about a place called Golem Creek?

DS: [coughing out large quantities of smoke] Fuck yeah. Like I was a ghost watching things happen. I got hold of Charley's confession—

MT: Wait. I thought you *wrote* that book. What the fuck, man? [reaches for joint]

DS: [toking up again before handing it over] Yeah, well. It's not like he's going to pay my fucking bills, you know? Yeah. I read it a couple of times and then wrote down what I could remember of it. You know, when I woke up. I think I got most of that shit right!

MT: [coughing]

DS: Anyway, Molly comes to me and she says—

MT: You met Molly Furnival?

DS: [takes a huge drag and nods vigorously]

MT: But isn't she the Færy Queen, or whatever the fuck it is you called her?

DS: [shrugs, grins, makes obscene gesture]

MT: So you're telling me—you're telling me that Molly's *real*, and you stole *Fear Club* from some guy that only exists in your imagination?

DS: Damn straight. [imitating villain from Scooby Doo] "And I would've gotten away with it, too, if it weren't for you meddling kids!"

MT: [hesitantly] This isn't—this is bullshit, right? What is in that grass, dude?

[sounds, as of something crashing through trees]

DS: Oh, Jesus Crutch. *No! It can't be*—

[chaos of noises]

MT: What're you doing?

DS: [cackling madly with laughter] Something I should've done a long time ago! [sound of chainsaw engine revving to life]

MT: Jesus CHRIST man! Put that fucking thing DOWN! AHHHHH!

DS: [hysterical laughter] *O Nox, Nox, qui celas infamiam infandi nefandi—ZOD-MANAS ZI-BA—*

[—tape ends—]

K
V
T
H

"THERE IS NO OTHER WAY"

XXIX

ADVERTISEMENT!

...the READER did it!!!

According to popular conspiracy theorist "Crazy" Jack Haines, Damian Stephens lives "at the edge of a dark forest in Virginia," etc., etc., but he's not going to be overly concerned about "oohing" and "aahing" everyone with all his clever little hyper-intellectual projects once certain vested interests discover he's published a number of their central secrets in a work of gutter-trash fiction. We suggest he find a place to hide and stay there.

— THE MGMT.